"I don't rememb**..**

he said.

She swallowed. "I'm not usually."

"So what has you strung so tight now?" he wondered aloud. "Are you worried that I'm going to make a move?" He took a step closer, so that she was trapped between the counter at her back and him at her front. "Or that I'm not?"

The pulse at the base of her jaw was racing, and her slightly parted lips—so tempting and soft—were mere inches from his own. Her gaze went to his mouth, lingered, as if she wanted his kiss as much as he wanted to kiss her.

Then she turned her head away and shifted to the left, sidestepping both him and the question.

"What's going on, Katelyn?" he pressed, because it was obvious that something was.

She nibbled on her bottom lip, her brow furrowed as if she was considering a response, but she said nothing as she pried the lid off the ice cream container.

"Katelyn?" he prompted, ignoring the caution lights that were flashing in his head.

Finally, she looked at him, her big blue eyes filled with worry. "I'm pregnant."

* * *

MATCH MADE IN HAVEN:
Where gold rush meets gold bands!

Dear Reader,

Welcome to Haven, Nevada, and to the first book in my new miniseries, Match Made in Haven!

I'm excited to be writing this new series for Special Edition and eager to introduce readers to the northern Nevada setting where the bachelors—and bachelorettes—are as untamed as the town's history.

The fictional County of Haven is sandwiched between (the very real) Humboldt and Elko counties, about thirty miles north of Battle Mountain. Apologies to Nevadans for liberties taken to create the setting for this series!

In Haven, readers will be introduced to a cast of new characters, including the Gilmores, who operate one of the most successful cattle ranches in the county, and the Blakes, who made their fortune mining gold and silver, as well as the ongoing feud between the two families. Of course, there are a lot of other interesting people around town, too—most notably sheriff Reid Davidson, who recently moved to Haven from Texas and, according to the whispers overheard at The Daily Grind, is already intimately acquainted with local attorney Katelyn Gilmore...

Of course, it's inevitable that the lawman and lawyer will find themselves on opposite sides in the courtroom, but the attraction that sizzles between them might be incentive enough to put aside their professional differences and realize that they are a Match Made in Haven.

I hope you enjoy their story and will return to Haven in June to find out if high school science teacher Alyssa Cabrera can find lasting chemistry with *Her Seven-Day Fiancé...*

All the best,

Brenda Harlen

The Sheriff's
Nine-Month Surprise

—

Brenda Harlen

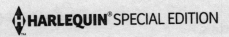

HARLEQUIN® SPECIAL EDITION

Recycling programs
for this product may
not exist in your area.

ISBN-13: 978-1-335-46561-0

The Sheriff's Nine-Month Surprise

Copyright © 2018 by Brenda Harlen

Printed in U.S.A.

Brenda Harlen is a former attorney who once had the privilege of appearing before the Supreme Court of Canada. The practice of law taught her a lot about the world and reinforced her determination to become a writer—because in fiction, she could promise a happy ending! Now she is an award-winning, RITA® Award–nominated national bestselling author of more than thirty titles for Harlequin. You can keep up-to-date with Brenda on Facebook and Twitter or through her website, brendaharlen.com.

Books by Brenda Harlen

Harlequin Special Edition

Those Engaging Garretts!

The Last Single Garrett
Baby Talk & Wedding Bells
Building the Perfect Daddy
Two Doctors & a Baby
The Bachelor Takes a Bride
A Forever Kind of Family
The Daddy Wish
A Wife for One Year
The Single Dad's Second Chance
A Very Special Delivery
His Long-Lost Family
From Neighbors...to Newlyweds?

Montana Mavericks: The Great Family Roundup

The Maverick's Midnight Proposal

Montana Mavericks: The Baby Bonanza

The More Mavericks, The Merrier!

Visit the Author Profile page
at Harlequin.com for more titles.

To #professionalromancefans—avid readers and tireless ambassadors of the genre.

With sincere appreciation.

Chapter One

Twenty-eight months

Katelyn Gilmore fell back onto the king-size mattress and drew in a long, deep breath as she stared up at the textured ceiling of the Courtland Hotel-Boulder City.

Twenty-eight months devoted exclusively to the establishment of her law practice, working long hours every day, including evenings and weekends, to prove herself to her clients and colleagues. Now, after twenty-eight months, she'd finally allowed herself to venture away from the office for a few days.

Okay, a conference wasn't actually a vacation, but the opportunity to hone her legal skills and enjoy a change of scenery was one that she couldn't refuse. And she was determined to enjoy the weekend—to get out of the hotel when the workshops had ended and breathe in some fresh air. Maybe she'd even take the time to see some sights, have a drink or two at a local bar, maybe flirt with a handsome cowboy—if she remembered how.

She enjoyed the company of men, and her sexual experiences—though limited—had been pleasant enough. Maybe not earth-shattering, but she didn't really believe that earth-shattering sex existed outside of books and movies. The truth was, she felt more anticipation when she was prepping for a trial than thinking about getting naked with a man.

"Which only proves you're getting naked with the wrong men," her sister had told her as she tucked a box of condoms in the suitcase Kate had packed for her trip.

Though Skylar was younger by five years, she had a much better understanding of the way a man's brain worked—and a lot more experience with other parts of the male anatomy.

Kate had removed the box and given it back to her sister. "I'm going to a legal conference at a five-star hotel, not an open house at a brothel."

"Still, you might luck out and meet a guy who is something more than a stuffed shirt," Sky had said, and returned the box to the niche she'd created between Kate's makeup bag and her underwear. "And even if you don't, it's better to be safe than sorry."

Because she agreed with her sister's last point, she'd left the condoms in her suitcase.

She also believed in careful planning and deliberation and wasn't the type of woman to act on impulse. Hooking up with a guy she met at a conference would be exactly that—and a little tawdry, too.

So when she hung up her suits and unpacked her other essentials, she left the condoms in her luggage, certain she'd have no need for them.

Certain...and maybe just a little disappointed.

* * *

Reid Davidson was sitting with his back to the wall and his eyes on the door when she walked into the conference room.

From a young age, he'd learned to be aware of his surroundings and the people around him—it was easier to dodge a backhand if he saw it coming—and the habit had served him well as the Sheriff of Echo Ridge, Texas.

But even if he hadn't seen her arrive, even if his head had momentarily been turned away, Reid would have been aware of her presence. She was the type of woman who snagged a man's full and complete attention and didn't let go.

She had bold blue eyes and sharp cheekbones in a heart-shaped face that was saved from looking prim by a lushly shaped mouth that promised the fulfillment of his wickedest fantasies. Her dark hair, shining with hints of gold and copper, was caught up in some kind of fancy twist that made him want to take out the pins and slide his fingers through it.

After pausing for a brief moment in the doorway, her gaze searching for an empty chair, she moved to the other side of the room with a brisk, confident stride that suggested she was a woman with important places to go and people to see.

Her body—long and lean with curves in all the right places—was buttoned up in a slim-fitting blue suit. The color was both lighter and brighter than navy and brought to mind the fancy glass his grandmother had collected. The skirt hugged her hips, and the matching jacket was fastened below her breasts with a single square button, above which peeked a hint of black silk.

He'd resigned himself to spending the weekend surrounded by lawyers and judges and other legal types. It wouldn't have been his first choice on how to spend three days, but the Echo Ridge town council strongly advocated continuing education for all its employees and, since that council was footing the bill for the weekend, he hadn't balked at the request.

He'd chosen to attend Sentencing Considerations in the Criminal Courts, believing it would be held in Boulder, Colorado, less than a two-hour flight from Echo Ridge. It turned out the conference was in Boulder *City*, which was in Nevada, adding another hour and another time zone to his travel. Although a potentially fortuitous error on his part, as he'd recently decided to move away from Echo Ridge and had, in fact, already applied to fill a vacancy in the Sheriff's Office in Haven, Nevada.

So he'd flown in a day early and made a quick trip to the northern part of the state to meet with the hiring committee before the conference. He'd been advised that a decision would be made before 4:00 p.m. Monday, and he figured the conference would distract him from counting the hours until then. As he watched the stunning brunette settle into her chair, almost directly across from him, he couldn't help but think that she would be an even better distraction.

She unzipped the top of her briefcase and removed a bottle of water, her cell phone and her iPad. If he'd been a betting man, he would have put money on her having been a straight-A student in school—the type who willingly sat at the front of the class to ensure she didn't miss a single word the teacher said.

The good girl had never been his type, and if he really wanted the distraction of a willing female to help get him through the weekend, he'd be better off hitting a club or the hotel bar when five o'clock rolled around. But his gaze lingered on the brunette, because it was a shame that a good girl should have a mouth that suggested it was capable of doing wonderfully bad things.

Now that she was set up, she turned to the balding man in the ill-fitting brown suit who was seated on her left. Making friends with her neighbors, he realized, when she said something, smiled and shook the man's hand. Then she turned to the woman on her other side, a skinny red-head with sharp eyes, and repeated the process.

Having finished with the introductions, she sat back in her chair. As more stragglers found their way to the room and filled the last few seats, she let her gaze move around the table. Then her eyes locked on his, and his stomach clenched as it absorbed the punch of sexual awareness.

He hadn't experienced anything like that in a long while, and he knew then that he wasn't going to walk away from her so quickly when the hour-long session was over.

Most of the seats were taken by the time Kate found the conference room where tables were set up around the perimeter to facilitate discussion. But she found a space between Lyle, a victims' rights advocate from Carson City, and Marcia, a former prosecutor-turned-defense-attorney from Fresno, California.

When she was settled in her chair, she let her gaze scan the room as last-minute arrivals squeezed into vacant seats. Her lazy perusal came to an abrupt halt when she saw him.

He was wearing a light gray micro-check shirt that stretched across mouth-wateringly broad shoulders with a loosely knotted plum-colored tie at his throat. His hair was brown, a few shades lighter than her own, and cut short. His forehead was high, his brows thick, his eyes—green? Brown? She couldn't quite tell from across the distance that separated them, but they were focused and intense. The bronze skin suggested that he spent a lot of time working or playing outdoors. The strong jaw, square and dark with stubble, gave him a slightly dangerous and yet somehow appealing edge.

There was no ring on the third finger of his left hand, resting casually on top of the table, but she knew that wasn't always proof of unmarried status. Then he caught her eye and winked boldly, and she felt heat spread up her neck and across her cheeks as she tore her gaze away. She was embarrassed to have been caught staring. She was also—unexpectedly and undeniably—aware of him on a purely visceral level.

It had been a long time since she'd been attracted to a man and even longer since she'd shared any kind of physical intimacy with one. She didn't know precisely how long, but it had been at least twenty-eight months because she hadn't been away from Haven in that period of time—and she definitely hadn't hooked up with anyone in her hometown. Heck, she couldn't even have coffee with a male colleague during morning recess from court without her sister texting to ask for details before her cup was empty.

So maybe it was the extended duration of her most recent dating hiatus that was responsible for her reaction to him. Or maybe it was his shoulders. Apparently she had a weakness for guys with great shoulders and strong jawlines and—

And somehow her errant gaze had drifted back to him again. Chiding herself for her reaction, she folded back the cover of her tablet and swiped to unlock the screen.

The moderator closed the door, effectively silencing the quiet murmur of conversation and focusing attention in his direction. After a brief introduction, he handed out some case studies for the participants to review and discuss.

As the debate evolved, Kate found herself arguing against the position taken by the broad-shouldered stranger who'd caught her eye. He insisted that adult crimes deserved adult punishment; she maintained that children didn't have experience making decisions or controlling their impulses and shouldn't be held to the same standards as their adult counterparts.

When the moderator finally called time on the session, neither of them had given an inch. And yet Kate found herself invigorated rather than frustrated, because while she didn't agree with her opponent's position, she had to admit that he'd made some good points and he presented his arguments in a rational and respectful manner.

As most of the other attendees funneled toward the door, he moved the other way—toward her. She took her time putting her materials away, pleased to note that her hands were steady despite the pounding of her heart. She uncapped her water bottle and tipped it to her lips to moisten her suddenly dry throat.

He wore jeans with his shirt and tie, and well-worn cowboy boots on his feet. Six feet two inches, she decided when she had to tip her head back to meet his gaze. And his eyes weren't green *or* brown but an intriguing combination of both. Hazel, she decided, though the word failed to describe the magnetism of his gaze. Tiny lines crinkled at the corners of his eyes and bracketed his mouth, and a thin scar slashed through his right eyebrow.

"Reid Davidson," he said.

She took the proffered hand—wide-palmed and strong—and felt a tingle of something dangerously tempting shoot up her arm and arrow toward her center. "Katelyn Gilmore."

"Defense attorney?" he guessed.

She nodded. "Among other things."

"Six months out of law school?"

She narrowed her gaze, not sure if his question was a legitimate guess or a subtle insult. "Four years."

He seemed surprised by that revelation. "Four years and you're not completely disillusioned yet?"

"My determination to fight for justice doesn't blind me to the flaws in our system."

"That's...admirable," he decided.

She slid the strap of her briefcase onto her shoulder. "You're a prosecutor," she guessed.

"No," he said quickly. Vehemently. "I'm not a lawyer."

"So what *do* you do, Not-a-Lawyer Reid Davidson?"

"I'm a sheriff."

She nodded, easily able to picture a shiny badge pinned to that wide chest. "And you throw the book at anyone who doesn't toe the line in your jurisdiction."

He didn't deny it. "It's my job to uphold the law."

"The law doesn't exist in a vacuum," she argued. "It requires context."

"Apparently you have some strong opinions on the subject," he noted. "Why don't we continue this discussion elsewhere, and you can enlighten me?"

She absolutely wanted to continue this discussion—or any discussion—if it meant spending more time with the broad-shouldered sheriff with the mesmerizing eyes and sexy smile.

"What did you have in mind?" she asked, determined to play it cool despite the anticipation racing through her veins.

"I could buy you a drink," he suggested.

She considered herself a smart woman—too smart to hook up with a stranger. But while she didn't know even the first page of Reid's life story, she knew that he set her blood humming in a way that it hadn't done in a very long time. And after more than two years without a man even registering a blip in her pulse, she was too curious to walk away without determining if the attraction she felt was reciprocated.

She wasn't looking for love. She wasn't even looking for sex. But she couldn't deny that she enjoyed looking at Sheriff Reid Davidson.

Sometimes you don't know what you want until it's right in front of you.

With the echo of her sister's voice in her ears, she made her decision. "A drink sounds good."

Reid had never been afraid to admit when he was wrong, and he'd realized—less than halfway through the workshop discussion—that he'd been wrong about her.

Katelyn.

The name struck him as a unique combination of the classic and contemporary, and as intriguing as the woman herself. Because while she might look prim and cool, there was a lot of heat beneath the surface. She argued not just eloquently but passionately, making him suspect that a woman who was so animated in her discussion of a hypothetical situation would be even more interesting up close and personal. Now he was about to find out.

There were two bars in the hotel—the first was an open lounge area that saw a lot of traffic as guests made their way around the hotel; the second, adjacent to the restaurant, was more remote and private. He opted for the second, where patrons could be seated at pub-style tables with high-back leather stools or narrow booths that afforded a degree of intimacy.

He guided her to a vacant booth. When the waitress came to take their drink order, Katelyn requested a Napa Valley cabernet sauvignon and he opted for a locally brewed IPA, signing the check to his room when the drinks were delivered.

After the server had gone, he raised his glass. "To stimulating discourse."

Though she lifted her brows at his deliberately suggestive word choice, she tapped the rim of her glass against the neck of his bottle.

"Where are you from, Sheriff Reid Davidson?" she asked, after sipping her wine.

"Echo Ridge, Texas."

"You're a long way from home," she noted.

"So it would seem," he agreed. "How about you?"

"Northern Nevada, so not quite such a long way."

"Humboldt, Haven or Elko County?"

"You must have aced geography in school," she remarked.

"I didn't ace anything in school," he confessed. "But I recently visited the town of Haven."

"Why were you there?" she asked, then held up a hand before he could respond. "No, don't tell me. I don't want to know."

"Why don't you want to know?"

"Because almost everyone in Haven knows everyone else—or at least knows someone who knows that someone else, and if it turns out that you hooked up with someone I know, this—" she gestured from her own chest to his and back again "—isn't going to happen."

"Is this—" he copied her gesture "—going to happen?"

She sipped her wine. "I'm thinking about it."

"While you're thinking, let me reassure you that I've never hooked up with anyone from Haven." His lips curved as he lifted his bottle. "Yet."

She set her glass on the table, her fingers trailing slowly down the stem. "You're pretty confident, aren't you?"

"Optimistic," he told her. "But I do need to ask you something."

"What's that?"

"Is there anyone waiting for you at home in Haven?"

"Aside from my father, grandparents, sister, two brothers, several aunts, uncles and cousins, you mean?"

"Aside from them," he confirmed.

"No, there's no one waiting for me." She traced the base of her wineglass with a neatly shaped but unpainted fingernail. "What about you, Sheriff Davidson—are you married?"

He shook his head. "Divorced."

"Girlfriend?"

"No," he said again. "Any more questions?"

"Just one," she said.

He held her gaze, waiting, hoping.

"Do you want to take these drinks back to my room?"

Chapter Two

Five weeks later

"I can't believe you're leaving." Trish Stilton pouted as she rubbed a hand over the curve of her hugely pregnant belly. "Especially now, only a few weeks before the baby's due to be born."

Reid dumped the entire contents of his cutlery drawer into a box. Though he didn't dare say it aloud, considering the imminent delivery of his ex-wife's baby, he'd decided that his timing was almost perfect.

"Just last week, I told Jonah that we should ask you to be the godfather, but now that you're moving to Nevada, that's out of the question."

Which further convinced Reid that he'd made the right choice in accepting the offer to take over the sheriff's position in Haven. Though he and Trish had been divorced for more than four years and she'd been remarried for almost three, they'd remained close. Maybe too close.

When she'd walked down the aisle to exchange vows with her current husband, Reid had been the man to give her away. Yeah, it had seemed an odd request to him, but he didn't see how he could refuse. When she'd found out that she was pregnant, she'd stopped at the Sheriff's Office to share the news with Reid even before she'd told her husband. And when she'd cried—tears of joy, because she was going to be a mother, mingled with grief, because her child would never know his grandfather—he'd held her and comforted her.

If she'd asked him to be her baby's godfather—as Jonah Stilton had warned him she intended to do—Reid wouldn't have been able to refuse. How could he refuse any request from the daughter of the man who'd saved his life?

Reid had been an orphaned teenager running with a bad crowd when the local sheriff took him under his wing. He didn't just turn Reid's life around, he saved it, and Reid knew there was no way he could ever repay the man who had been his mentor, father figure and friend. So when Hank realized he wasn't going to beat the cancer that had invaded his body and he'd confided to Reid that he was worried about his daughter, Reid had promised to take care of her. The news of their engagement had been a balm to the older man's battered spirits, and he'd managed to hold on long enough to see Reid and Trish exchange their vows.

"I'm honored that you thought of me," he said to his ex-wife now. "But I'm sure your baby's father would prefer to have his brother fill that role."

"Jonah understands how important you are to me," she said, without denying his claim.

"You're important to me, too, but I think this move is going to be the best thing for all of us."

"But why do you have to go so far away?" she demanded.

"Nevada's not all that far," he said soothingly.

"But Haven?" she pressed. "I looked it up—it might as well be called Nowhere, Nevada, because that's where it is."

"Then I won't expect you to visit," he said mildly.

"Of course, I'll visit," she promised. "Because you don't have any friends or family in that town."

"Actually, I do have a...friend...in Haven."

"A female friend?" she guessed.

He nodded.

"I *knew* there had to be another reason that you suddenly decided to leave Echo Ridge—something more than a temporary job."

"She's not the reason I'm leaving," he said truthfully. "But I am looking forward to seeing her again."

"What's her name?"

Reid shook his head. "None of your business."

Trish smiled. "Afraid I'll track her down and ask about her intentions?"

"Yes," he admitted.

Not that he was really worried. He had no doubt that Katelyn Gilmore could handle his ex-wife. But the attorney had no idea that he was moving to Haven, because they hadn't exchanged any contact information before they went their separate ways after the conference. And with the perspective that came with time and distance, he couldn't help but wonder if he'd made the weekend they'd spent together into more than it really was.

"Well, it would only be fair," Trish said now. "You wouldn't let me go out on a second date with Jonah until you'd done a complete background check on him."

"Because your father asked me to take care of you," he reminded her.

"He wanted us to take care of each other," she said.

And for a while, they'd done just that. But Trish had wanted more than he'd been willing or able to give her—an *irreconcilable difference* that led to the end of their marriage. When that happened, he felt as if he'd let down Hank as much as Trish, but he knew his old friend would be pleased to see his daughter in a committed relationship with a man who could give her everything Reid couldn't.

He was sincerely happy for her, because she was happy. For himself, he'd decided a long time ago that he wasn't cut out to be a dad. A kid who'd been knocked around by his mother's various boyfriends for the first six years of his life, then raised by his widowed grandmother for the next eight before being kicked into and around the system didn't know anything about being a father. He'd lucked out when he'd met Hank. Trish's father had given him an idea of the type of man a dad should be, but Reid suspected it was too little too late, that the scars from his earlier years were too numerous and deep to ever truly heal.

"Now you've got Jonah," he reminded her.

"Yes, I do," Trish said, smiling through the tears that filled her eyes again.

"Jeez, will you stop with the waterworks?" he demanded, passing her a box of tissues.

She plucked one out and dabbed at her eyes. "I can't help it—it's pregnancy hormones."

"Well, let your husband deal with your blubbering—he's the one who knocked you up."

"Yes, he did," she said proudly, rubbing a hand over the enormous swell of her belly. "And those hormones have also led to doing a lot more of what got me into this condition."

He lifted his hands to cover his ears. "Way too much information, Trish."

She laughed through her tears. Then she reached out

a hand to touch his arm. "Can I give you one piece of advice?"

"Can I stop you?" he countered drily.

She ignored his question. "Before you get involved with this woman—before *she* gets involved with you—be honest about what you want and don't want from a relationship."

"I never meant to be dishonest with you," he said quietly.

"I know," she admitted. "The problem was, we rushed into marriage without ever talking about all the things we should have talked about."

He nodded. "But now you have everything you wanted."

"Soon," she amended, rubbing a hand over her baby bump again. Then with her other hand, she grabbed his and drew it to the curve of her belly. "Do you feel that? He's kicking."

He did feel it, little nudges against his palm. He wondered if it hurt her, to have a tiny human being moving around inside of her, but that seemed like too personal a question to ask. Not that his ex-wife seemed to care about boundaries, which was why Reid was moving out of state in an effort to establish some. Instead he asked, "He?"

Trish smiled and nodded. "It's a boy. We're going name him Henry—for my dad."

Reid had to clear the tightness from his own throat before he could respond. "That's a great name."

She watched him tape the flaps of the box shut. "I really wish you weren't going."

He hadn't expected that his ex-wife would make this easy for him, but he hadn't expected that it would be so hard, either. But he didn't—couldn't—waver. He needed to move on with his life, and as long as he was living a stone's throw away from her, he knew that wouldn't happen.

"You're going to be okay, Trish. You don't need me anymore."

She sniffed and knuckled away a tear that spilled onto her cheeks. "But what if you still need me?"

She'd been his family—his only family—for seven years now. But it didn't matter if he still needed her—it was time for him to move on.

Kate thanked the clerk as she slid the judge's signed order into her client's file, tucked the file into her briefcase and turned away from the desk. She exited the courthouse, pausing outside the doors to perch her sunglasses on her nose in defense against the bright afternoon sun, then continued on her way. She'd been told that she moved purposefully, like a woman on a mission, and she usually was.

Today her mission was to get away from the courthouse before she threw up. She crossed the street and ducked into the shade of the trees that lined the perimeter of Shearing Park. The greenspace was usually quiet at this time of day, offering the privacy she needed. She lowered herself onto the wooden slats of a bench and reached into her briefcase for the sleeve of saltine crackers she'd been carrying for the past few days.

She inhaled, taking three long deep breaths. Then she nibbled on a cracker and sipped some water. When she felt a little steadier, she pulled out her cell phone and dialed her office.

"I've got the custody order for Debby Hansen," she said when her assistant answered the phone. "If you want to print up the cover letter and final account so everything's ready to go, that would be great. I'm heading to a settlement conference in Winnemucca this afternoon, but I'll be back in the office in the morning."

She could picture Beth frowning at Kate's schedule on

her computer screen. "I don't have anything about a set-tlement conference."

"I set it up myself—a favor for a friend," she explained. *Lied.*

If she was looking in a mirror, she would see flags of color on her cheeks. Thankfully, Beth wasn't able to see the telltale proof of her deception.

"Okay," the other woman said agreeably. "I'll leave your docket and the files for tomorrow morning on your desk before I lock up."

"Thanks, Beth."

She disconnected the call and nibbled on another cracker. She'd never felt good about lying, but lately she'd been doing a lot of it.

Lying to her assistant, to explain her absences from the office. To her dad, when he said she looked peaked. To her sister, when Sky asked what was wrong. To her grand-mother, when she hinted that Kate was working too hard.

To herself, when she suggested that the first home preg-nancy test was faulty and there was no reason to panic.

It was only when a second, and then a third, test showed the same obviously inaccurate result that she'd decided to see an ob-gyn.

She tucked her crackers back into her briefcase, walked to her car and headed toward Battle Mountain. Because she would rather drive thirty-five miles out of town than risk the inevitable speculation that would follow a visit to a local doctor.

"Good afternoon, Ms. Gilmore—I'm Camila Amaro."

Kate accepted the proffered hand of the woman who entered the exam room. "Thank you for squeezing me in."

"You sounded a little panicked on the phone."

"I'm feeling a little panicked," she admitted.

The doctor didn't go behind her desk to sit down but

leaned back against it, facing her patient. "Is this your first pregnancy?"

She managed a weak smile. "So much for thinking the results of three home pregnancy tests might be wrong."

"False results do happen," the doctor acknowledged. "But a false positive is extremely rare, and the test we ran here confirms the presence of hCG—the pregnancy hormone—in your system."

"I'm really pregnant? I'm going to have a baby?"

"You're really pregnant," the doctor confirmed.

She'd dreaded receiving this confirmation. How could she possibly juggle her professional responsibilities with the demands of a baby? And yet, something surprising happened when the doctor said those three words. She felt a loosening of the knots in her stomach and unexpected joy in her heart.

A baby.

And she knew then that it didn't matter that she hadn't planned for this—she would figure out a way to make it work.

"Do you want to set up a sonogram so we can establish how far along you are and discuss the options that are available to you?" Dr. Amaro asked.

"Five weeks and six days," Kate told her.

"You're sure?"

She nodded. "Broken condom."

The doctor opened the folder she carried and made a note in the file. "Are you in an exclusive relationship with the father?"

The question was matter-of-fact and without any hint of censure, but Kate felt her cheeks flush with embarrassment that she'd been so foolish and careless. A weekend fling had seemed like a good idea at the time—some harmless fun to break the monotony of her everyday life. She'd never anticipated that a few unforgettable nights would give her a lasting reminder of those nights with the handsome sheriff from Texas.

"No," she admitted. "In fact...I haven't seen him since the weekend that we were...together."

"Then maybe we should run some other tests?" the doctor suggested gently.

She wouldn't have thought it was possible, but her already burning cheeks flamed even hotter. She'd been so off-kilter about the possibility of a pregnancy that she hadn't given a thought to any other potential consequences of unprotected sex.

Of course, when the condom broke, she and Reid had talked about their respective sexual histories to reassure one another that there was no cause for alarm. But she nodded her assent to the doctor now. "Yes, please. Whatever you need to do—I want to know that my baby's going to be okay."

"Then you do want to have the baby?" Dr. Amaro asked in the same neutral tone.

Kate nodded again. While she appreciated the woman's professional manner and obvious determination not to influence her decision, there had never been any question in Kate's mind. Even when she'd still been firmly in denial about the possibility of a pregnancy, she'd known that—if she was pregnant—there was no other choice for her but to have the baby.

She'd always wanted to have a family...someday. Of course, she'd expected to be more established in her career—and preferably married—before that dream became a reality, but she was going to play the hand that had been dealt and be the best mother she could be to her baby.

She had no intention of making any claims on Sheriff Reid Davidson of Echo Ridge, Texas. She'd gone to bed with him not just willingly but eagerly, and even if the possibility of a pregnancy had never entered her mind, she alone had chosen to have this baby and she alone would be the responsible for that choice.

And while she had no idea how he would respond to the news that he was going to be a father, she knew that she had to tell him.

Soon.

Chapter Three

Reid stared at the modest pile of boxes in the middle of his new kitchen. He suspected that most people, by thirty-four years of age, had acquired more stuff, but when he and Trish had separated, he'd moved into a fully furnished apartment and let her keep the house and almost everything in it.

While looking at the housing options in Haven, he'd found an in-law suite available to rent only a few blocks from the Sheriff's Office—furnishings available—and decided that was again the easy option. Glancing around his new home, he acknowledged that he should have asked for photos.

Whether or not his decision to move to Haven, Nevada, would prove to be the right one had yet to be determined. But he'd needed a fresh start, he'd liked what he'd seen of the town on his first visit and he'd been assured by Jed Traynor, the former sheriff who had been forced into early retirement by some health concerns—and his wife—that Haven was populated by mostly good people.

And then, of course, there was the Katelyn factor.

He wasn't foolish enough to let his career decisions be influenced by a weekend fling, no matter how spectacular and unforgettable the sex had been. But he'd been thinking about her a lot and he was looking forward to the opportunity to see her again.

Seeing her naked again would be even better.

She was a woman of intriguing contrasts. When she'd walked into the conference room, she'd been the picture of cool professionalism, but it hadn't taken long for him to realize how much heat simmered beneath the surface. The passion she'd displayed in advocating her position in the conference room was just as evident in the bedroom.

She'd made the first move—not just when she'd invited him back to her room, but when she'd kissed him. There had been nothing tentative about that first kiss. No questions or doubts about what either of them wanted. Their mouths had come together eagerly, almost desperately.

They'd both been enthusiastic participants in their lovemaking. Tearing at their own clothes while simultaneously trying to undress each other, laughing when limbs got tangled in uncooperative fabric.

When she'd been stripped down to a tiny pair of black bikini panties and a low-cut bra, he'd stopped laughing.

Hell, his heart had almost stopped beating.

She was so incredibly hot.

So wonderfully agile.

So totally willing.

And even six weeks after only two nights together, he hadn't forgotten any of the details of the time he'd spent in her bed. Not the way her eyes went dark when she was aroused or the soft, sexy sounds that emanated from deep

in her throat. Not the rosy pink buds of her nipples or
the tiny brown mole beside her belly button. Not the way
her hair looked fanned out on the soft pillow behind her
head, or the erotic brush of those long tresses as her lips
leisurely explored his body. Not the way her thighs quiv-
ered when he stroked deep inside her or the way her inner
muscles clenched around him when she finally succumbed
to her climax.

Yeah, he was definitely looking forward to seeing her
again.

With that thought in mind, he decided to abandon his
unpacking for a while and wander the neighborhood—to
get his bearings. At least that would be the justification if
anyone asked. The truth was, he'd already located the most
important places: Sheriff's Office; courthouse; Diggers',
the neighborhood bar and grill; Jo's, a local pizza place;
The Trading Post, the general store; and, a few blocks
down from the courthouse, The Law Office of Katelyn
T. Gilmore.

Her practice was set up in a beautiful old building with
a cornerstone that established the date of its erection as
1885. Maybe the old library, he speculated, since Jed had
pointed out the new community center, which included a
swimming pool, gymnasium, "the new library," several
multipurpose rooms and administrative offices.

"Are you in need of legal counsel?"

Reid turned to face a woman who appeared to be in her
mid- to late-sixties, about five-four with shoulder-length
dark hair liberally streaked with gray, wearing a plaid shirt
with faded jeans and well-worn boots.

"No, ma'am," he said. "Just admiring the building."

"The old library," she said, confirming his supposition.
"It was built in 1885, as were most of the buildings on this
stretch of Main Street, but the doors didn't open until 1887.

It's rumored that sixteen-year-old Elena Sanchez hid out in the basement of this very building for three weeks in the fall of 1904 to avoid being forced to marry."

"Did she succeed?"

The woman nodded. "With the help of the librarian, Edward Jurczyk, who sneaked in blankets and food for her. Two years later, they were married. Nine years after that, Edward was killed fighting in The Great War in Europe."

"Haven has quite an interesting history," he mused, his gaze returning to the wide front window where Katelyn T. Gilmore was painted in bold black letters outlined in gold and Attorney at Law was spelled out below in slightly smaller letters.

"Katie opened her office here almost two-and-a-half years ago," the woman continued. "If you're ever in need of an attorney, you couldn't do better. She sometimes has office hours on weekends, but she's out of town right now."

"You seem to know a lot about Ms. Gilmore's schedule," he noted.

And sharing more information than you should with a stranger, he wanted to caution. Of course, he kept that admonition to himself, as he was eager to hear anything about Katelyn that she was willing to tell him.

"Of course, I do," she replied. "Katie's my granddaughter."

"I'm beginning to believe that everyone in town knows—or is—a Gilmore." He offered his hand. "I'm Reid Davidson, the—"

"The new sheriff," she finished for him, as she gripped his hand in a surprisingly firm shake. "I know who you are. And I'm Evelyn Gilmore, not some dotty old woman who would spill personal information about my family to a stranger on the street."

Then her gaze narrowed speculatively. "So you apparently know that Haven was founded by the Gilmore family," she acknowledged, "but what do you know about the Blakes?"

He forced his expression to remain blank. "Who?"

She laughed. "It might turn out that you're exactly what this town needs, Sheriff Reid Davidson. You plan on staying beyond the completion of your current term?"

"Maybe you should table that question until after I've actually started my job," he suggested.

"Maybe I will," she decided. "Until then, if you've got time for a cup of coffee, I can introduce you to Donna Bradley. She's been working the counter at The Daily Grind for longer than it's been The Daily Grind.

"Cal's Coffee Shop, it used to be called," she continued. "But Cal died nearly a dozen years ago now and when his granddaughter took it over, she gave it a face-lift and a new name. She was smart enough to keep Donna, though, and if there's any news in town, she's usually the first to know it."

"I've always got time for a cup of coffee," Reid said, looking forward to her commentary on the community and its residents—and hopeful that she'd share more information about Katelyn.

Though Kate had been feeling tired for a couple of weeks, having the doctor explain that fatigue was normal in the first trimester, because her body was expending lots of energy helping to grow a baby, seemed to exacerbate the situation. By the end of the following week, she was really dragging.

Thankfully, she didn't have court Friday morning, but she did have an appointment at the community center in the afternoon to talk to a group of seniors about wills and estate planning. After the session was finished, she decided to call it a day.

Her cell phone rang just as she pulled into the parking lot behind the old library, which housed not only her law office but her apartment above it. Shifting her vehicle into Park, she glanced longingly at the second-floor windows. If she ignored the ringing, she could have her shoes off and her feet up in less than three minutes.

She answered the call, anyway.

"Hey, Kate—it's Liam," her brother said, as if she wouldn't recognize his voice or the number on the display.

"What's up?" It was unusual for him to contact her in the middle of the day, so she knew his call had a specific purpose.

"Do you remember my friend, Chase, from school?"

"Of course," she said.

"Well, I just got off the phone with his brother, Gage, who called me because Chase told him that my sister is an attorney."

"Are you getting to a point anytime soon?"

"Yeah," he said. "Gage's son, Aiden, has been arrested."

Now *that* was a surprise.

Aiden wasn't just a good kid, he was unfailingly honest. The type of kid who wouldn't swipe a pack of chewing gum from The Trading Post. In fact, Kate remembered a time when he'd paid a dollar for ten gummy worms but Samantha Allen, who was working behind the counter, miscounted. When Aiden realized he'd been given eleven candies, he tried to give one back.

"What did he allegedly do?"

"I don't know," Liam admitted. "I didn't think to ask, but Gage is panicking because he's still half an hour out of town and he wanted to know if there was anything you could do to help."

"Okay," Kate decided. "Tell him to bring Aiden in to see me tomorrow morning. I have a couple of later appointments but I should be able to squeeze them in around eleven."

"This can't wait until tomorrow. Aiden's being held for a bail hearing—that's why Gage is so frantic."

"He's a juvenile with no prior record," Kate said, thinking aloud.

"Can you find out what's going on?" Liam asked.

"I'm on my way to the Sheriff's Office right now," she promised.

She parked her vehicle then walked the few blocks to the Sheriff's Office. Judy Talon, the administrative assistant, was seated behind the front desk.

"Hey, Katie—are you here about Aiden Hampton?"

She nodded. "But I don't have any of the details," she admitted. "Can you fill me in?"

Judy glanced at the sheriff's closed door but still dropped her voice when she said, "He was arrested with Trent Marshall."

Under normal circumstances, they both knew that Aiden Hampton didn't keep company with kids like Trent Marshall—and he definitely didn't get in trouble with the law. Unfortunately, nothing had been normal for Aiden since his grandmother had died a few weeks earlier.

"What did they do?"

"Found a car with the keys in the ignition and decided to take it for a spin."

"Joyriding," she realized.

"Some would say," Judy agreed. "The new sheriff is saying grand larceny of a motor vehicle."

"You've got to be kidding."

The other woman shook her head. "I wish I was."

"Grand larceny is a felony."

"Which is why he's being held over for a bail hearing," Judy explained.

"Obviously, Jed didn't tell his replacement how things work around here." Kate glanced at her watch. "What time is the hearing?"

"Ten a.m. Monday morning."

"Oh, no." She shook her head. "I'm not letting Aiden spend the weekend in lockup."

"I hope he doesn't have to," the other woman agreed, though her tone was skeptical.

Kate looked toward the office. When Jed had run the department, the door was almost always open. Now it was closed, and she hoped that status wasn't a reflection of the sheriff's mind. "Can you let the new sheriff know that I need a few minutes of his time?"

Judy picked up the phone to connect with the sheriff, but first whispered, "Good luck."

She didn't let the woman's words unnerve her. After giving a perfunctory knock on the door, she turned the knob.

Be confident. Be convincing. Don't back down.

She repeated the refrain inside her head as she stepped into the office.

Be confident. Be convincing. Don't—

The rest of the words slipped from her mind as familiar hazel eyes lifted to meet her gaze.

And she found herself face-to-face with her baby's daddy.

Reid had been looking forward to the day when he would see Katelyn Gilmore again. He didn't anticipate that it would happen as soon as his third day behind the desk in the Sheriff's Office.

He'd been writing a report when she walked in, and he automatically glanced up—and was immediately sucker punched by her presence.

If the sudden widening of her eyes and the sharp intake of her breath were any indication, Katelyn was just as surprised to see him. Maybe even more so, because while he'd known their paths would cross and had eagerly anticipated that eventuality, it appeared that she'd been unaware of the identity of Haven's new sheriff.

"Reid?"

"Hello, Katelyn." He thought he'd remembered how beautiful she was, but seeing her again proved his memories inadequate.

She was wearing another one of those lawyer suits, this one a deep purple color with a pale pink shell under the jacket, which made him wonder what color lace she might be wearing beneath that. Her hair was pinned up as it had been the day of their first meeting, but he knew now how it felt when he slid his fingers through it as he kissed her. And maybe that wasn't a memory he should linger on while he was wearing his official sheriff's uniform, because the mental image was causing his body to stir in a very unprofessional way.

She opened her delectably shaped and incredibly talented mouth, then closed it again without saying another word.

"You're Aiden Hampton's attorney?" he prompted.

She nodded. "And you're the new sheriff."

"I am," he confirmed.

"But...I thought you lived in Texas. I even—" Now she shook her head. "It doesn't matter."

"What doesn't matter?"

She ignored his question to ask her own. "Why are you here?"

"I applied for the job before I met you," he said, wanting to dispel any concern she might have about his motivation. "In fact, I interviewed with the hiring committee the day before the conference in Boulder City."

Her cheeks flushed as she cast a quick glance at his open office door.

He nodded to the phone on his desk, indicating the light that revealed his assistant was occupied with a call.

"When I told you that I was from Haven, why didn't you mention that you'd applied for a job here?"

"Because you didn't want to know," he reminded her.

Her brows drew together as she recalled that earlier conversation and finally admitted, "I guess I did."

"And when I got the call offering me the job, well, I figured our paths would cross soon enough."

"They're going to cross frequently if you insist on locking up juveniles who should be released on their own recognizances."

He leaned back in his chair. Though he was disappointed that she'd so quickly refocused on her client, he could appreciate that she had a job to do. Any personal business could wait until after-hours. "Grand larceny of a motor vehicle is a felony."

"Grand larceny of a motor vehicle is a ridiculously trumped-up charge."

"Tell that to Rebecca Blake—it was her brand-new S-Class Mercedes, worth close to two hundred thousand dollars."

That revelation gave her pause, but just for a second. "Was the vehicle damaged?"

"Thankfully, no," he acknowledged.

She nodded, and he could almost see her switching mental gears from confrontation to persuasion. "He's a good kid, Reid—a straight-A student grieving for his grandmother."

He wouldn't—couldn't—let sympathy for the kid interfere with his responsibilities. "There are lots of kids who lose family members and don't act out by stealing a car."

"Elsie Hampton helped raise Aiden from birth, after his mother walked out of the hospital without her baby, leaving him in the custody of his seventeen-year-old father. But of course, you didn't know that, did you?"

"How could I?" he countered.

"You could have asked someone," she told him. "Everyone in Haven knows his family and his history. In fact, his dad works with Jed's son at Blake Mining."

He gave a short nod. "Point taken."

"So I can take my client home now?"

"No," he said.

"Why not?" she demanded.

"Because I've already gone on the record stating that he's to be held over for a bail hearing."

She sighed. "Then you're going to have to call Judge Calvert and ADA Dustin Perry and tell them you want to have a bail hearing."

"While I appreciate your passionate advocacy, Katelyn, you don't make the rules around here—I do."

"I get that you're new," she said. "Not just new to this office but new in town, and you might think I'm trying to manipulate you for the sake of my client, but I'm not."

"Well, okay, then," he said, making no effort to disguise his sarcasm. "I'm sure the judge and the prosecutor will both be thrilled to be called out to a bail hearing at four thirty on a Friday afternoon."

"I'm sure they won't be," she countered. "But they'd be even less happy to find out, on Monday morning, that you made Aiden Hampton spend the weekend in a cell."

"If I agree to do this, it will look like your client got preferential treatment," he warned.

"No, it will look like the new sheriff finally took his head out of his butt for a few minutes."

Though her blatant disrespect irked him, Reid couldn't help but admire her passion and conviction.

"Your client was processed by the book," he told her.

"Maybe," she allowed. "*If* he'd actually committed grand larceny of a motor vehicle, but the reality is that he went for a joyride—and joyriding is a misdemeanor offense."

"A gross misdemeanor," he clarified.

"Are you going to make those calls or should I, Sheriff?"

"Are you really trying to put my badge between us now, Katelyn?"

"Seems like you were the one who did that," she said. "And it's Kate. Everyone here calls me Kate."

"Or Katie," he noted.

She frowned. "Only my family calls me Katie."

"I like Katelyn better, anyway."

She huffed out a breath. "The judge and ADA?" she prompted.

He picked up the phone.

Thirty minutes later, all parties were assembled at the courthouse. Less than half that time had passed again before Aiden Hampton was released into the care of his grateful and relieved father.

The assistant district attorney didn't stick around any longer than was necessary to sign the papers. The judge didn't even wait that long. After enumerating the usual conditions for release, he gave the new sheriff a brief but pointed speech about the value of the court's time and suggested that he familiarize himself with the way things were done in Haven, because apparently it was different than what he was used to.

Kate didn't let herself feel sorry for Reid. But she did appreciate that he'd called the hearing, albeit reluctantly, and she said so as they walked side by side out of the courthouse. "Thank you."

"The next time I put your client in a cell, he's going to stay there a lot longer," Reid warned.

"There won't be a next time," she said. "Aiden really is a good kid who chose the wrong way to work through some stuff."

"By hanging out with a friend already on probation?"

"I don't know what he was doing with Trent Marshall," she admitted. "They don't usually run in the same circles."

"I'm guessing you represent the Marshall kid, too?"

She nodded. "And I'm curious as to how the kid already on probation walked away with a summons to court and the kid who's never been cited for jaywalking ends up locked in a cell."

"If you really want to know, I'll tell you—over dinner."

Chapter Four

Kate's mind was reeling. Not just because she was once again in close proximity to the sheriff, with whom she'd had the Best. Sex. Ever. a few weeks earlier, but because she now had to accept that the father of her baby wasn't fifteen hundred miles away but living in the same town.

"Dinner?" she echoed, and realized it could be the perfect opportunity to share her big—and growing—news.

"Traditionally the third and biggest meal of the day," he explained, amusement dancing in those hazel eyes.

"I understand the term," she assured him. "I was just... surprised...by your invitation."

"Surprised is okay," he decided. "But are you hungry?"

She realized that she was. The queasiness that left her feeling unsettled through most of the morning usually disappeared by lunch, and lunch had been a long time ago.

"I could eat," she finally responded to his question, determined not to allow the sexy sheriff's nearness stir other appetites.

"Good," he said. "I'd like to buy you dinner, but I'm going to ask you to decide where since I'm still finding my way around town."

"There are only three places in this town where you can get a decent meal," she told him. "The Sunnyside Diner, which does a great all-day breakfast but isn't so great with other menu options, Jo's Pizza, which makes the best thin crust pizza I've ever had—and their wings are pretty good, too—but eating in means nabbing one of only half a dozen tables crammed into a tiny space and no hope of a private conversation, and Diggers'."

"I've been to Diggers'," he told her. "The food was great."

"It is," she confirmed. "But we can't go there."

"Why not?"

"Because Diggers' is second only to The Daily Grind for gossip in Haven."

"You're worried people will talk about us sharing a meal?"

"I don't want to have to answer questions about how I'm acquainted with the new sheriff," she admitted.

"What's wrong with the truth?"

She shook her head. Now more than ever, she didn't want anyone to know that she'd met Reid in Boulder City, because when her pregnancy became apparent and people started counting backward, they'd suspect the baby had been conceived while she was out of town and she'd rather they didn't know that Haven's new sheriff had been there, too.

"Actually, I was referring to the other truth," he said. "That our paths crossed when you came to my office."

Which was a perfectly reasonable explanation. As an attorney, it made sense that she'd want to cultivate a good relationship with the new sheriff. But she also knew that if she was seen in public with him, it would be all the excuse anyone else wanted or needed to interrupt their conversation to wrangle their own introductions.

"Except that it's Friday."

"And?" he prompted, obviously seeking clarification.

"And my sister, Skylar, works at Diggers' on the weekend," she admitted.

"We could pick up pizza and take it back to my place," he suggested as an alternative.

She hesitated. "Look, Sheriff, despite what happened between us in Boulder City, I'm really not that kind of girl."

"You're not the kind of girl who likes pizza?"

She managed a smile. "I'm not the kind of girl who goes back to a guy's place—or invites him back to hers."

"I wasn't expecting to share anything more than pizza," he said, then shrugged. "Hoping, maybe, but not expecting."

The honest response undermined her resolve. "Why don't I make something for dinner instead?" she impulsively offered.

"I'd never say no to a home-cooked meal."

"I'm not promising anything fancy," she warned. "But you'll be able to eat and we'll be able to talk without a thousand interruptions."

"That works for me," he agreed.

She glanced at her watch, then mentally calculated the time she needed to make a quick trip to The Trading Post before she could start cooking. "Seven o'clock?"

"Sure," he agreed.

"Okay, I'll see you then."

He caught her arm as she started to turn away. "Only if you give me your address."

"Do you know where my office is?"

"You live at your office?"

"Above the office. Apartment 2B."

"I'll see you at seven."

Inviting Reid to have dinner at her place seemed like a good idea at the time—or, if not a good idea, at least a necessary compromise. They needed to talk and she didn't want to have the conversation where anyone might overhear it. But now that he was here, Kate realized she'd made a tactical error.

She loved her apartment—the ultramodern kitchen and open-concept living area with tall windows looking down on Main Street, two spacious bedrooms and a luxurious bathroom. Certainly, it had never seemed small—until Reid Davidson stepped inside. He wasn't a man whose presence was in any way, shape or form subtle, and it was as if he filled every square inch of space with his potent masculinity.

Being near him had her hormones clamoring so loudly she could barely hear herself think. And while her mind was desperately trying to focus on certain facts that needed to be discussed, her body was stirring, aching, wanting.

She took the bottle of wine he offered, and as her fingertips brushed against his, she was suddenly reminded of the way those fingers had touched her—the bold confidence of his hands as they stroked over her body, taking her to heights of pleasure she'd never even imagined.

He'd changed out of his sheriff's uniform and into a navy polo shirt that stretched across his broad shoulders. The hem of the shirt was tucked into a pair of softly faded jeans that hugged his lean hips and strong thighs, as her legs had hugged those hips and thighs, their naked limbs tangled and their bodies moving together.

She set the bottle of wine on the counter and turned to

dump the pasta in the pot of boiling water on the stove, hoping the steam would explain the sudden flush in her cheeks.

"Did you want wine or beer or something else?"

"I'd love a beer if you've got one handy," he said.

She stirred the pasta, then moved to the refrigerator to retrieve a bottle of Icky IPA. "Bottle or glass?" she asked as she pried off the cap.

"Bottle's fine."

Instead of taking the bottle she offered, he wrapped his hand around hers.

"What are you doing?" she asked warily.

"Trying to figure out why you invited me to dinner but haven't made eye contact since I walked through the door."

She lifted her gaze to meet his. "I'm just trying to get dinner finished up."

"Tell me what I can do to help," he suggested.

Go back to Echo Ridge.

The response immediately sprang to mind, but of course, she couldn't say the words aloud without then explaining why his sudden and unexpected appearance in Haven complicated her life.

Instead, she only said, "For starters, you could give me back my hand."

He loosened his grip so that she could pull her hand away without dropping the bottle. "What else?"

She gestured to the living area. "Go sit down."

"You don't trust me to help?"

"There's really nothing you can do," she told him.

"Do you want me to open the wine?"

She shook her head. "I'm going to stick with water— I've got work to do tonight." Which was true, if not the whole truth.

He took his beer and moved around to the other side

of the island. But instead of retreating to the living area and relaxing on the sofa, he chose one of the stools at the counter.

"So what do you think of Haven so far?" she asked, resigned to making small talk for eight minutes while the pasta cooked.

"I like it," he said. "It's a little smaller than Echo Ridge, but there's a strong sense of community here."

"There is," she confirmed, lowering the heat on the burner beneath the sauce. "Even when I was away at school, I knew I'd come back here after graduation."

"Summa cum laude from UCLA Law."

She frowned. "How'd you know that?"

"I met your grandmother," he confided.

"How? When?"

"Last weekend. I was walking down Main Street, trying to get a feel for the town, and our paths crossed. We had coffee together."

"You had coffee with my grandmother?"

He nodded. "She introduced me to Donna Bradley at The Daily Grind."

"You had coffee with my grandmother," she said again.

He studied her as he tipped his bottle to his lips, swallowed. "Why does that bother you?"

"It doesn't bother me," she denied. "But it's a little weird."

"Why?"

"Because she's my grandmother and you're…"

"The guy you had lots of naked sweaty sex with?"

"Okay, yes," she allowed.

"I didn't tell her about the naked sweaty sex," he promised.

"Thank you for that," she said drily.

He just grinned.

And that smile did strange things to her pulse…or maybe it was the heat from standing so close to the stove.

"But I haven't stopped thinking about it—or you," he continued. "I applied for the job before I met you, but you were definitely a factor in my decision to accept it."

"We weren't ever supposed to see one another again," she reminded him of the agreement they'd made in Boulder City.

"And yet, you went to Echo Ridge last weekend." The surprise must have shown on her face because he explained, "You left a message with Deputy Ryker."

She nodded. "A friend of mine from law school lives in Texas. Since I was there, I thought I'd stop by to say hi."

"Texas is a pretty big state."

"Chloe lives just outside of Dallas, so a side-trip to Echo Ridge wasn't really out of my way."

"Oh," he said, sounding disappointed. "I was kind of hoping you'd made the trip to see me."

The timer on the stove buzzed, granting her a temporary reprieve from the increasingly awkward conversation.

"Dinner's ready."

There was something on her mind.

Something more than concern about the client who'd brought her into his office a few hours earlier. When Luke Ryker told him that she'd shown up at the Sheriff's Office, he'd hoped it was memories of the nights they'd spent together that inspired Katelyn to track him down. But she certainly wasn't giving the impression of a woman motivated by carnal desires.

And though she kept up her end of the conversation while they ate, her thoughts were obviously elsewhere.

"Is it convenient or tiresome to live above your office?" he asked, attempting to engage her attention.

Katelyn twirled her fork in her pasta. "It's convenient," she said. "Certainly a lot more convenient than driving twenty miles into town from the Circle G Ranch every day."

He'd heard of the Circle G—reputedly the biggest and most prosperous cattle ranch in all of Haven County. It was also, if he remembered the story correctly, half of the property that was the original source of friction between the Gilmore and Blake families when they settled in the area more than one hundred and fifty years before.

According to local folklore, back in the spring of 1855, a developer sold a 100,000-acre parcel of land in Nevada to Everett Gilmore, a struggling farmer from Plattsmouth, Nebraska. The same developer also sold 100,000 acres to Samuel Blake, a down-on-his-luck businessman from Omaha. Both men subsequently packed up their families and their worldly possessions and headed west for a fresh start.

Everett Gilmore arrived first, and it was only when Samuel Blake showed up with his deed in hand that the two men realized they'd been sold the exact same parcel of land. Since both title deeds were stamped with the same date, there was no way of knowing who was the legitimate owner of the land. Distrustful of the local magistrate's ability to resolve the situation to anyone's satisfaction—and not wanting to publicly admit that they'd been duped—the two men agreed to share the property between them, using the natural divide of Eighteen-Mile Creek as the boundary between their lands.

Because the Gilmores had already started to build their home in the valley—on the west side of the creek—the Blakes were relegated to the higher elevation on the east, where the land was mostly comprised of rocky hills and ridges. The Gilmores' cattle immediately benefitted from grazing on more hospitable terrain, while the Blakes struggled for a lot of years to keep their herd viable—until silver and gold were found in the hills on their side of the creek and they gave up ranching in favor of mining.

"Is there any truth to that story about the ancestors of the Gilmore and Blake families coming to Nevada to settle the same piece of land?" he asked her now.

"It's all true," she assured him. "The Gilmores still own the fifty thousand acres on the west side of the creek and the Blakes own the fifty thousand acres, including all the gold and silver, on the east."

She put her fork down and picked up her glass of water. "You were going to tell me why Trent was given a court date and Aiden was locked up," she reminded him.

"Because Trent was a passenger in the car that Aiden was driving."

"Where'd they find the car?" she asked.

"Parked, with the key in the cup holder, in the driveway of the owner's house on Mountainview Road."

Katelyn shook her head. "Anyone who leaves, in plain view, the key to a fancy car deserves to have it stolen."

"I'll pretend I didn't hear you say that."

"How mad was Rebecca Blake when she realized her car had been taken?"

"Beyond mad," he admitted. "And more than a little embarrassed, because she knew that she'd left the key in it."

"She was at Elsie Hampton's funeral—and she's known Aiden since he was in diapers," Katelyn told him. "As mad and embarrassed as she was, I'm a little surprised that she wanted to press charges."

"It wasn't her choice," he said.

"You do know you'll never get a conviction on grand larceny, don't you? It would be a waste of time and resources to even take it to trial."

"That's an argument better saved for your discussions with the prosecutor," he suggested.

"Maybe it's different in Echo Ridge, but here the prosecutor doesn't usually make decisions about the disposition of charges without first consulting the Sheriff's Office."

"I investigated the complaint of a stolen vehicle and made the appropriate arrests," he said. "Now it's up to your pal in the ADA's office to decide what to do with the defendants."

"Dustin Perry's not my pal," she told him.

"I saw the two of you chatting while waiting for the judge. He seemed...favorably inclined toward you."

"You know, for a guy who was quick to point out that he's not a lawyer, you sound an awful lot like one at times."

He frowned. "Are you trying to spoil my appetite?"

She looked at his almost empty plate. "Not much chance of that."

"What can I say? This is great pasta," he said.

And it was. The red sauce had chunks of tomato, pepper and onion and was just a little bit spicy. But while he'd been mopping up sauce with a second slice of crusty bread, he noticed that she'd hardly touched her meal. She had her fork in hand and was pushing the pasta around on her plate, but she'd rarely lifted the utensil to her mouth.

"I didn't make anything for dessert, but I do have ice cream," she told him.

"What kind?"

She pushed her chair away from the table and went to open the freezer drawer below the refrigerator. Her appliances were all top of the line—as was everything else that he could see. Whoever had renovated the building had spared no expense in the dark walnut cupboards, natural granite countertops, marble tile and hardwood floors.

"Chocolate, chocolate 'n' peanut butter or chocolate chip cookie dough," she offered.

"Nothing with chocolate?" he asked drily.

A smile tugged at the corners of her mouth as she shrugged. "Sorry."

"Do you have cones?"

"No, but I have waffle bowls," she told him.

"Even better," he decided.

"What kind do you want?"

"Cookie dough."

She took the container out of the freezer and set it on the counter, then opened the cupboard and stood on her toes. "If they were more easily accessible, I'd indulge all the time," she explained, as she stretched toward the top shelf.

"If you didn't want to indulge, you wouldn't buy them," he commented, easily reaching over her head for the box.

She pulled open a drawer to retrieve an ice-cream scoop. "That's just the kind of logic I'd expect from a man."

He set the box on the corner, then lifted his hand to tuck an errant strand of hair behind her ear, his fingertip slowly tracing the outer shell.

The scoop slipped from her grasp, bounced on the counter.

"I don't remember you being skittish," he said.

She swallowed. "I'm not usually."

"So what has you strung so tight now?" he wondered aloud. "Are you worried that I'm going to make a move?" He stepped closer, so that she was trapped between the counter at her back and him at her front. "Or that I'm not?"

The pulse at the base of her jaw was racing, and her slightly parted lips—so tempting and soft—were mere inches from his own. Her gaze went to his mouth, lingered, as if she wanted his kiss as much as he wanted to kiss her.

Then she turned her head away and shifted to the left, sidestepping both him and his question.

"What's going on, Katelyn?" he pressed, because it was obvious that *something* was.

She nibbled on her bottom lip as she pried the lid off the ice-cream container.

"Katelyn?" he prompted, ignoring the caution lights that were flashing in his head.

Finally, she looked at him, her big blue eyes filled with wariness and worry. "I'm pregnant."

Chapter Five

She hadn't intended to blurt it out like that, but now that the words had been spoken, Kate actually felt relieved. It was no longer this big secret that she was keeping bottled up inside; she'd done the right thing and told Reid about the baby.

Now she just had to deal with his reaction, whatever that might be.

He reached behind him, his hands curling over the edge of the island countertop, as if he needed the support to remain standing. She understood how he felt—she was more than a little unsteady herself.

She moistened her lips with the tip of her tongue, waiting for him to say something, anything.

"You're sure?" he asked, after a long minute had passed.

She nodded. "I took one of those over-the-counter tests. Actually, I took three," she admitted. "And I got official confirmation from the doctor last week."

He went back to the table for his beer, tipped the bottle to his lips. "That's why you were in Echo Ridge," he realized. "Because you think it's mine."

Her cheeks burned with embarrassment, but she couldn't fault him for asking. She'd jumped into bed with him only a few hours after their first meeting—why wouldn't he assume that was normal behavior for her?

"I know it's yours," she told him. "You're the only man I've been with in…a long time. But considering how quickly everything happened between us, I can understand why you'd ask, why you'd want proof."

He fell silent again, and she found herself babbling in an effort to fill the silence.

"We can have a DNA test as soon as the baby's born. It's possible to do paternity testing before birth, through amniocentesis, but it also increases the risk of miscarriage and I'd rather not take the chance when there are no other factors that warrant it."

He nodded, but whether it was in agreement or understanding, she had no idea.

"I'm not asking anything of you," she hastened to reassure him. "I made the decision to have this baby on my own, and I intend to raise the baby on my own."

That, finally, got a response from him.

"You didn't make the baby on your own," he pointed out.

"Well, no," she agreed, her body humming in remembrance of the pleasures she'd experienced in his arms.

"And I don't shirk my responsibilities," he said with grim resolve.

"I appreciate that, Reid, but—"

He shook his head. "No buts, Katelyn."

She didn't know him well enough to have anticipated his response to the news—whether he'd be shocked or angry or disbelieving, but she'd tried to prepare for all those possibilities. So far, he hadn't responded with any recognizable emotion.

"I think we both need to take some time to think about what this means and where we want to go from here," she suggested cautiously.

Finally, he nodded. "That's probably a good idea."

She exhaled a quiet sigh of relief as she followed him to the door.

He paused with his hand on the knob. "If you need anything, give me a call."

"I will."

Then he leaned down and touched his lips to the top of her head. "Thanks for dinner, Katelyn."

The sweet gesture made her throat tighten. She closed her eyes against the sudden sting of tears as she shut the door behind him and flipped the lock.

Only eight days had passed since Dr. Amaro had confirmed her pregnancy, after which her first thought had been to track down Reid and let him know that she was going to have his baby. Traveling all the way to Echo Ridge only to discover that he wasn't there had been another emotional upheaval. She'd been filled with disappointment and frustration and, yes, relief.

It was as if she'd been given a reprieve, an opportunity to figure out what she wanted to do without having to factor her baby's father into the equation. Finding him in the Sheriff's Office in Haven was just one more surprise she hadn't been anticipating.

Working in family law had shown her that co-parenting could make things a lot easier—or a lot harder. She also knew that if Reid wanted to acknowledge paternity and be a father to their child, there was nothing she could do to stop him.

Was it any wonder that she was feeling exhausted and overwhelmed and terrified?

Because if he didn't want to be involved, she'd have to struggle through every step on her own. Not just pregnancy and childbirth, but midnight feedings, diaper rashes and teething woes. Then skinned knees and long division and, in later years, first dates and broken hearts and various other disappointments.

But she was equally terrified that he'd embrace fatherhood and she'd have to interact with him on an almost daily basis for the next eighteen years and beyond. The recent trend toward shared custody meant that he could be entitled to equal time with the baby who was right now nestled in the warm comfort of her womb. He would have an equal say in where their child went to school and what sports or activities he or she participated in.

And maybe they'd be in complete agreement about all those things—but what if they weren't?

She touched a hand to her still-flat stomach, awed and amazed to think that there was a tiny life growing inside her. A tiny life that would someday call her mama, then mommy and mom and eventually mother, accompanied by a preteen eye-roll.

She had no experience of her own to draw on after that. Theresa Gilmore had died when Kate was twelve, forcing her to negotiate the awkward teen years and all major transitions after that without her guidance. There were so many milestones that she'd marked without her mother's presence: graduation from high school, acceptance to law school, the unveiling of her name stenciled on her office window.

There were so many times over the years that she'd missed having her mom around, but never had she missed her support more than she did upon realizing that she was going to be a mother herself. And now, she was going to have to go through all the phases of pregnancy and child-birth without her, too.

Still, Kate knew she was lucky. Though her father wouldn't be happy to learn that his unmarried daughter was going to have a baby, she didn't doubt that he'd be supportive—or that he'd love his grandchild. Her grand-parents and sister and brothers would also be there any time she needed anything. And her best friend, Emerson, a recent new mother, would be able to offer advice and insights.

Despite all the support available to her, she was scared to death that she'd somehow screw this up.

And because her baby had been conceived with a man she barely knew, she'd have to work with him to figure out what was best for their child.

Oh, what a mess I've made of my life.

Except that she didn't really regret anything that had happened, because she already loved her baby more than she'd ever thought possible.

Returning to the kitchen to tidy up the dishes, she noticed the forgotten chocolate chip cookie dough on the counter. She dropped the unused scoop back in the cutlery drawer and took out a spoon. Then she sat down on the cold tile floor and dipped her spoon into the tub.

Because melting ice cream was at least one problem she knew how to solve.

Reid left her apartment with no concept of where he was going or what he was going to do.

Katelyn Gilmore was pregnant—with his child—and he was completely unprepared to be a father.

It wasn't just bad timing. He wasn't one of those guys who always thought he'd be a father "someday" but had to accept that the day would come sooner than anticipated. No, years earlier Reid had consciously decided that he wouldn't ever have a child. He'd even considered having surgery to ensure it couldn't happen, except that the prospect of going under the knife was daunting and condoms were readily available.

But fate had apparently decided to kick that conscious decision to the curb. It was as if all the stars had aligned to screw him over with a broken condom.

Not that he'd ever put much stock in fate or the alignment of stars, but when his ex-wife had met her current husband, she told Reid that fate had put Jonah in her path. He'd countered with skepticism, pointing out that the hand of destiny—if there was such a thing—had better things to do than muck around in the computers at 4evermatch.com. Trish would no doubt get a huge kick out of his current predicament, claiming it was karma because he'd disrespected the higher powers of the universe.

Not that he intended to tell Trish—or anyone else. At least not until he and Katelyn had figured out what they were going to do.

For now, he just started walking. He didn't want to go home. He didn't want to be alone, because then he'd have to think about the news Katelyn had dropped in his lap. He'd have to acknowledge that, all conscious decision-making and careful planning aside, he was going to be a father.

He walked with no clear destination in mind, past the shops and businesses that lined Main Street. He lifted his hand in greeting when Reggie Mann—owner and operator of Mann's Movie Theater—called out to him, but he didn't pause. He didn't want to make conversation; he didn't want to make friends.

What he wanted, he realized as he approached Diggers' Bar & Grill, was to get so rip-roaring drunk he could no longer hear the words that continued to echo in his head. Of course, he'd never let the residents of Haven see their sheriff in such a state, but he was off duty and out of uniform, so he figured it was okay to have a drink or two.

The double doors opened into an enclosed foyer that housed two entrances. The one on the left was clearly marked Bar and the one on the right designated Grill. Once inside it was easy enough to move from one side to the other, as both were under the same roof with only a partial wall dividing them, but it allowed families to take their kids for a meal without having to walk through a bar to get to a table.

The interior was deliberately rustic, with floors of unpainted, weathered wood slats, scuffed and scarred from the steady traffic of boot heels. Framed newspaper headlines proclaiming the discovery of gold and silver in the nearby hills hung on the walls along with miners' helmets, metal pans, buckets, coils of rope, pickaxes and a few other items that he had no idea what they were but hoped were securely fastened, because some of them had the potential to be lethal weapons otherwise.

Reid's first day on the job, Jed Traynor had taken him through the door on the right to Diggers' Grill for lunch. Tonight, he went through the door on the left.

There were several patrons already seated at the bar— some of them watching the baseball game on the two big screens, a young couple snuggled close together sharing a plate heaped with cheesy nachos, a trio of older men focused on their drinks.

He straddled a vacant stool and surveyed the labels on the taps in front of him. Not that it really mattered which one he chose—after a few, they all tasted pretty much the same. And his only purpose in being here right now was to drink until his brain was fuzzy enough to let him forget he was going to be a dad.

The irony of the situation was not lost on him. His marriage had fallen apart because he didn't want to have a child with his wife. Now he was going to have a child with a woman he barely knew. And while the situation wasn't what he would have chosen, Katelyn's pregnancy took choice out of the equation.

Maybe it's not mine.

The thought sneaked into his mind, seductively tempting.

But over the years, he'd gotten adept at reading people, and nothing Katelyn had said or done had given him reason to suspect she wasn't being honest with him.

I know it's yours. You're the only man I've been with in...a long time.

And if he needed any more evidence that he could plausibly be the father of her baby, there was the broken condom.

That had created a moment of panic for both of them, but they'd managed to convince themselves that the odds of a faulty bit of latex coinciding with her fertile time were negligible. And they'd put the broken condom out of their minds and made love several more times after that, without any further mishaps, unable to get enough of one another. He hadn't been so hot for any female since he was a teenager and the sight of Lana Doucet in skintight jeans and a clingy sweater was enough to give him a hard-on.

But there was something about Katelyn—from the minute she'd walked through the door of that conference room, he'd wanted her. He'd been sure it was his lucky day when she agreed to have a drink with him. When she invited him back to her room, he'd felt like the luckiest man in the world.

Apparently his luck had run out.

One of the bartenders, an attractive blonde with blue eyes and an easy—almost familiar—smile, made her way down the bar. Reid studied her for a minute, wondering if he'd already met her in town. If he had, he couldn't remember when or where.

"What can I get for you?" she asked.

"I'll have a pint of the Sierra Nevada Pale Ale."

She grabbed a glass from the shelf but paused before setting it under the tap. "Are you sure you don't want something stronger?"

"What?"

"You've got the look of a man who needs a shot—or two dozen—of strong whiskey."

He'd never been the type to turn to the bottle, but he'd never been faced with a situation of such magnitude. "Maybe you're right," he acknowledged. "What do you recommend?"

She replaced the glass and selected a bottle, holding it up for his approval.

Reid nodded and she poured a generous two fingers of Maker's Mark into a whiskey glass, then set the drink on a paper coaster in front of him. "Anything you want to talk about?"

He shook his head. He not only wasn't ready to talk about Katelyn's disclosure, he didn't want to think about it. But even if he wanted to talk, he knew better than to say a word to anyone in this town where everyone seemed to know the Gilmore family.

"I've been told that I'm a good listener," the bartender said to him, her smile encouraging.

"By anyone who wasn't drunk?"

She laughed. "As a matter of fact, yes."

"Well, I have a confession… I've never been told that I'm a good talker."

"Maybe this will help," she said, and poured him another drink.

He stared at the amber liquid in his glass, tempted to throw it back. Then another and another. Until he finally managed to drown out the echo of Katelyn's voice in his head.

I'm pregnant. I'm pregnant. I'm pregnant.

"Do you have a name? Or should I just call you Mister-Not-A-Good-Talker?" the bartender asked.

"Reid," he said.

"Are you new in town, Reid, or just passing through?"

"New in town," he said.

"From...Texas?" she guessed.

He nodded.

"Which would make you the new sheriff."

He nodded again.

"Well, you're a definite upgrade from the old sheriff," she remarked. "I mean, Jed's a nice guy and all, but when women sigh over a man in uniform, they aren't sighing over men like Jed. But you, on the other hand—yeah, women would sigh over you."

He looked up from his drink. "Are you flirting with me?"

"Me?" She seemed genuinely surprised by the question. "No." Then, more emphatically. "God, no."

He lifted a brow.

"Sorry," she said. "I didn't mean to sound quite so vehement, I just didn't realize that you would assume... Although now that I'm replaying the words in my mind, of course you assumed I was flirting with you. But the truth is, I was thinking about someone who hasn't sighed over a man in a long time." She shook her head. "Now it sounds like I'm covering up for my own fumbling attempts at flirting with you, and I'm not, and I'm sorry if I've made you uncomfortable."

"You haven't," he assured her.

"But now I have a question that might," she warned. "What's your relationship status?"

"My relationship status?"

She nodded. "Are you married, engaged or otherwise involved?"

"If you're not flirting with me, how is my relationship status at all relevant?" he wondered.

"I'll tell you the relevance if you tell me your status."

"Are you sure you're not flirting with me?"

"You're cute, Sheriff, but you're not my type. You are, however, the type of guy I can imagine my sister totally going for."

"Thank you, I think. As for my relationship status… there might be a wedding in my not-too-distant future."

"That sucks," she said. "Oh—not for you, of course. It's great for you. But it's not easy to meet guys in this town, especially when your last name is Gilmore, and Katie hasn't had a date in… I don't even know how long."

"Wait a minute." Reid held up a hand. "Did you say your last name is Gilmore?"

She nodded.

"And your sister's name is Katie—or Katelyn?"

She nodded again, confirming his suspicion that everyone in town knew the Gilmores—or *was* a Gilmore.

"Then you must be Skylar."

Her gaze narrowed suspiciously. "How would you know that?"

"Because I know your sister."

"You do?"

"In fact—" he lifted his glass of whiskey, as if making a toast "—she's the woman I'm going to marry."

Chapter Six

Kate was already in her pajamas when her cell phone chimed to announce a text message. She wanted to ignore it. She wanted to burrow under the covers and fall into a deep and dreamless sleep to forget—for at least a few hours—that her entire life was about to change.

Of course, she couldn't do that—at least not without checking the message first to ensure it wasn't a family emergency or a client crisis or anything else that required an immediate response. She paused the baseball game on TV and picked up her phone.

She felt a quick spurt of panic when she read the message and keyed a quick response. Then, after exchanging her pajama bottoms for a pair of yoga pants and tugging a hoody over her T-shirt, she headed out.

Eight minutes after leaving her apartment, she was walking into Diggers'.

Haven was only one of three cities in the whole state of

Nevada where gambling was prohibited, which meant that weekends saw a regular exodus of residents who sought more exciting opportunities than those available within city limits. For those who opted to stay, Diggers' was a popular destination.

Tonight, the local watering hole was doing a brisk business, with most of the seats at the bar occupied. Right now, Kate's sister was simultaneously pouring drinks, taking cash and flirting with several customers. A lot of people knew Dave Gilmore's youngest daughter worked weekends as a bartender at Diggers'—only a handful knew that she was a masters candidate who tended bar not just for tips and fun but to observe human behavior.

Kate spotted Reid right away, sitting between Oscar Weston, a local mechanic who was sipping his usual Budweiser straight from the bottle, and a couple of younger guys sipping scotch, neat, and arguing over the validity of the umpire's call in the same baseball game she'd been watching at home. Despite the presence of other patrons around him, it was apparent that Reid was alone and wanted to be that way.

She squeezed herself between the stools and leaned an elbow on the bar. "Hey, Sheriff."

"Katelyn?" He blinked at her, as if he was having trouble focusing. "What are you doing here?"

"I got a text from my sister, asking me why a drunk guy at the bar believed he was going to marry me." She kept her voice low to ensure their conversation wouldn't be overheard.

"Because I am," he asserted. "And I'm not drunk."

She looked at the empty whiskey glass on the coaster in front of him. "How many of those have you had?"

"Three?" He nodded his thanks to Skylar when she set a mug of coffee in front of him. "I was celebrating."

"What were you celebrating?"

"My impending nuptials," he said, the relatively co-herent pronunciation suggesting that he wasn't as inebri-ated as she'd feared. On the other hand, his brain had to be addled by alcohol if he was thinking a wedding was anywhere in their future. "Not only am I getting married, but I'm going to be—"

She pressed a hand to his mouth, anticipating and si-lencing the rest of his words.

"It's a secret?"

She nodded and let her hand drop away.

He lifted the mug to his mouth, watching her over the rim as he sipped his coffee. "You are so incredibly beauti-ful. I thought I remembered what you looked like, but when you walked into my office… Was that today? Yesterday?"

"Today," she confirmed.

"When you walked into my office today, you took my breath away."

"Are you sure you've only had three whiskeys?"

He swallowed another mouthful of coffee. "Pretty sure," he said. "And though I wouldn't attempt to operate a motor vehicle right now, I promise I haven't had enough alcohol to impair my vision."

"Finish your coffee," she suggested. "And I'll take you home."

He dutifully picked up the cup again. "I've been think-ing about you for weeks," he confided. "Dreaming about you."

She shot a quick glance to the left and then the right, but no one seemed to be paying any attention to their con-versation.

"In fact, I haven't stopped thinking about you since you walked into that conference room in Boulder," he continued. Then he shook his head. "No, it was Boulder City, wasn't it?"

She rolled her eyes. "And now you're in Haven, and I need to know where you live so I can get you home."

"133 Chicory Drive."

She was familiar with the street and mentally placed the number. "Norm and Beverly Clayton's place?"

He nodded. "I'm renting the basement apartment."

Which Kate knew had been an in-law suite where Beverly's mom had lived for a lot of years. After she broke her hip and needed to go into a long-term care facility, Norm and Beverly had periodically offered the space for rent.

"Let's get you back there and into bed," Kate suggested.

"If you want me in bed, you only need to ask."

She shook her head, but she couldn't hold back the smile that curved her lips. "Even drunk you can't turn off the charm, can you?"

"Am I charming the pants off you?"

"You already did," she reminded him. "That's why you were trying to drink yourself into oblivion."

Reid didn't tell her again that he wasn't drunk. He just paid his tab, adding a generous tip for the bartender, and let Kate lead him away.

She automatically turned south when they stepped out of the bar. "Where'd you park?"

"I didn't drive, I walked."

He stopped in the middle of the sidewalk. "You're not walking me to my apartment, then walking back, alone, to yours."

"Reid, I've lived in Haven my whole life—I have no concerns about being out on my own after dark."

"But you thought I needed an escort home?"

"Sky's message led me to believe that you were more intoxicated than you apparently are."

"Now that you know I'm not, I'll walk you home," he decided, turning in the opposite direction.

"Fine," she agreed, falling into step beside him. "We'll walk back to my apartment and then I'll drive you to yours."

She turned at the corner of Page Street, then again into the parking lot behind her building. She hit the button on her key fob to unlock the doors, then climbed behind the wheel as he went around to the passenger side of the SUV.

"Why'd you come to the bar?" he asked.

"Because if you get stumbling-down drunk, people are going to gossip and speculate, and I'll feel responsible."

"Why would you feel responsible?" he asked.

She started the car and pulled out of her parking space. "Because I turned your world upside down tonight."

"Yeah, you did," he acknowledged. "And I turned yours upside down by launching super swimmers into your fallopian tubes."

She laughed softly as she turned onto Second Street. "I have to admit, I've never heard the fertilization process described in quite that way."

"I'm just trying to point out that we're both responsible for what happened—and the consequences."

"You're right," she said. "But I can't help wondering if you might have made a different decision about coming to Haven if you'd known I was pregnant."

He shook his head. "I wouldn't have made a different decision," he assured her. "I wouldn't—I don't—want to be anywhere else.

"Well, except maybe a different apartment," he acknowledged as she pulled into his driveway.

"What's wrong with the apartment?" she asked.

He just shook his head. "You have to see it to believe it."

Her gaze narrowed suspiciously. "If you're trying to get me into your bedroom…"

He shook his head. "It's the living room—and the kitchen—you have to see."

She turned off the ignition.

He led her to the side of the house, where there was a separate entrance to his apartment, and unlocked the door.

Kate was still wary, but she followed him inside.

"It's very open," she noted. "Lots of space and natural light. And the decor is…interesting."

"I was looking for a place that was furnished," he explained. "And although I'm not actually allergic to flowers, I want to sneeze every time I walk in here."

She nodded. "There are a lot of flowers."

It wasn't just that the sofa and chairs were covered in bold floral fabrics, but the coffee table, end tables, desk, filing cabinet and lamps were all painted with cabbage roses and daisies and tulips.

"I heard that Beverly took a tole painting class a few years back," Katelyn told him. "I didn't realize how much she obviously enjoyed it."

"There are flowers everywhere," he said. "The kitchen table is covered—I thought it was one of those doily things and figured I could fold it up and put it in the linen closet. But it's painted right on."

She went through the living area to the kitchen to examine the table.

"It's really very well done," she noted, tracing a finger along the delicate edge of the "lace."

"I don't know how long I can live like this," he confided.

"Some women like a man who's in touch with his feminine side."

"I'd rather be in touch with a woman's feminine side."

His response was so predictably defensive, she couldn't help but smile. "Why does that not surprise me?"

"You have a really great smile," he told her. "Every time you smile at me…even when you're not smiling, every time I see you… I don't know how to describe what happens inside me, but I look at you, and I want you."

"You're definitely feeling the effects of that whiskey now," she said, unwilling to admit—even to herself—the powerfully seductive effect his words had on her.

"Why are you so determined to deny what's between us?"

"The only thing between us is the baby that resulted from a broken condom."

"Do you really believe that?"

There was something in his tone, just the slightest hint of an edge that should have set off warning bells in her head, but she was so determined to prove her point, she ignored the signs. "It's true, Reid, what happened in—"

That was as far as she got before his mouth came down on hers.

And if he was under the influence of the alcohol he'd drunk, it certainly didn't affect his aim or impact his skill.

The first time they'd kissed, she'd discovered that Reid was a patient and thorough man. Kissing wasn't just foreplay to him but an incredibly sensual experience that turned her on more than she'd ever thought a kiss could do.

The same focus and skill that had seduced her then was seducing her now. The rational part of her brain told her that this shouldn't be happening, but all rationality was drowned out by the clamoring needs of her body.

She hadn't consciously parted her lips, but suddenly his tongue was dancing with hers, leading it in a sensual rhythm that promised more, so much more. Liquid warmth began to spread through her body, pool between her thighs.

His hands slid under her hoody and skimmed up her

sides. She could feel the heat of his touch through the thin fabric of her T-shirt. His palms brushed the sides of her breasts, and paused when he realized she wasn't wearing a bra.

She held her breath, waiting to see what he would do next. She knew what she *should* do—push him away, say good-night and walk out the door. But her brain and her body clearly wanted different things, and it had only taken one kiss to remind her of the pleasures she'd experienced in his arms. Pleasures she wanted to experience again.

Suddenly his hands were stroking boldly over her bare skin, stoking the fire that was already burning inside her. His callused thumbs scraped over her nipples, making her gasp as arrows of pleasure shot to her core.

He tore his mouth from hers only long enough to yank her hoody and T-shirt up and over her head and toss them aside. Then he was kissing and touching her again, and it was all she wanted, but somehow not enough.

Desperate to touch him as he was touching her, she tugged his shirt out of his jeans and let her hands explore the rippling muscles of his stomach, chest and shoulders. There was just something about those shoulders that made her crazy.

His lips eased away from hers to rain kisses along her jawline…down her throat…across her collarbone…over the curve of her breast. Then they fastened around her peaked nipple and drew it into his mouth, and her knees almost buckled. But Reid's arm was around her back, holding her close. Her fingers dug into his broad, strong shoulders so hard her nails had to be scoring his skin. He merely shifted his attention to the other breast.

"Reid."

It was all she said, all she could manage with so many wants and needs battering at her from all directions.

He lifted his head from her breast, but his hands immediately took over where his mouth had left off, teasing and tweaking the hard buds. In the past few weeks, she'd noticed that her breasts were a little more sensitive than usual—a not uncommon effect of early pregnancy. Apparently they were even more sensitive than she'd realized, because Reid's touch had pushed her almost to the point of climax.

"Do you have any idea how much I want you?" he asked.

She could feel the press of his erection against her belly, and the answering heat spread through her veins, making her eyes cross. "I hope it's half as much as I want you."

His eyes, hot and dark, locked on hers.

"If you're going to tell me to stop, you better say it now," he warned.

She could only shake her head. "I don't want you to stop." She slid a hand between their bodies, stroking him through denim. "I want you."

He sucked in a breath. "You're killing me here, Katelyn."

"Don't tell the sheriff." She tugged on his belt. "He'll lock me up."

"That scenario does hold some appeal," he admitted.

She nibbled on his bottom lip. "Let's get you out of these clothes," she suggested, carefully working the straining zipper over the bulge of his erection.

"And you out of yours," he agreed.

Of course, she was just wearing yoga pants, so he had the easier task. He hooked his thumbs in the waistband and slid them over her hips and down her legs.

"You said you didn't want to go near my bedroom," he reminded her.

"And I wouldn't want to be accused of lying," she said, tumbling with him onto the sofa.

There was laughter and frustration as he tried to wriggle out of his clothes with her body draped over his, but eventually they were both naked and panting, desperate for one another.

"Katelyn—"

She didn't know what else he was going to say, but she suspected she didn't want to hear it, so she took a page out of his book and silenced his words with her mouth. She kissed him long and slow and deep, and while she was kissing him, she positioned her knees on either side of his hips, then eased her lips from his and pulled back so that his erection was poised at the juncture of her thighs.

She was hot and wet for him, her insides trembling with the anticipation of taking his hard length deep inside her, but apparently she still had a few working brain cells because she hesitated. "I know there's no point in worrying about birth control but—"

"I haven't been with anyone else since we were together," he told her. "I haven't wanted anyone but you. But I do have condoms in the—"

He stopped talking when she tilted her hips. She took the tip of him inside her...then a little bit more. Deliberately drawing out his pleasure...and her own. Until he was finally...completely...deeply...inside her.

She closed her eyes, relishing the sensations that were zinging through her system like a thousand tiny little balls inside an out-of-control pinball machine.

Reid gave her a minute to adjust to his size and presence, then he lifted his hips, moving inside her. Slowly at first, establishing an even and steady rhythm...then faster...harder. And those erotic sensations continued to build and multiply until...it was too much.

And everything inside her shattered.

Chapter Seven

Reid woke up naked and alone.

He was sprawled on the flowered sofa with his clothes strewn around the floor, proof that his recollection of the previous evening was more than a dream.

If he'd had any doubts that his memories were hotter than the reality of getting naked with Katelyn, last night's sofa sex had laid them to rest.

Unfortunately, waking up and finding her gone suggested that they still had some issues to resolve. Remembering that she was pregnant multiplied those issues and amplified the importance of finding a resolution.

He made his way to the bathroom, cranking up the hot water in the shower in the hope that it would help clear some of the cobwebs from his brain. He braced his forearms on the ceramic tile as the spray pounded against his back, and he acknowledged that nothing could change the simple and basic facts:

Katelyn was pregnant.

And he was the father of her baby.

Since the idea of drinking himself into oblivion hadn't succeeded, he needed a plan B.

Unfortunately, the only possible fix he could see for this impossible situation was marriage. He vaguely recalled mentioning the idea to Katelyn last night—and that she'd responded with little enthusiasm.

He wasn't exactly thrilled by the prospect, either, but he didn't see any other choice. He'd been taught to take responsibility for his actions, even—and especially—when the consequences were uncomfortable. And marrying the mother of his child was the right thing to do.

He was still freaked out about the idea of being a father—a job for which he had no skills and even less experience—but he could see only one path forward. Maybe it was old-fashioned to want his son or daughter to grow up with two parents, but that was what Reid wanted for his child. The very thing he himself had been denied.

Which meant that he had a major task ahead: convincing Katelyn to marry him.

Kate woke up in her own bed and wanting coffee—desperately.

Dr. Amaro had assured her that she didn't need to give up caffeine completely but had suggested that she cut back to twelve ounces a day. Kate honestly didn't know how much she usually drank—she'd never worried about keeping track before. Her first cup was always at home in the morning, to help kick her brain into gear as she got ready for work, and throughout the day, there was usually a cup within arm's reach on her desk. If she was in court, recess meant a quick trip to the courthouse café for a vanilla latte. But since she'd vowed to reduce her caffeine intake, she'd been starting her mornings with a cup of herbal tea instead. She had yet to find a flavor that put her in a good mood to start the day. Today's pick—lemon ginger—was supposed to help combat nausea, but it had a distinctly medicinal taste that wasn't at all appealing. She took another sip and made a mental note to pick up some decaf coffee later. She'd never understood why anyone would drink decaf—what was the point of coffee without caffeine?—but under the circumstances, she thought she might give it a try.

In the meantime, she was going to have to sort out the mess she'd made of her life without the boost of caffeine.

Every decision she made from now on had to take into account not only what she wanted but what was best for the baby she was carrying. She had no idea how sex with Reid fit into that equation. Obviously getting naked with him had been a mistake, even if it had felt really good at the time.

Which wasn't something she should be thinking about right now, so when Sky walked in, Kate was so grateful for the distraction that she didn't think to wonder what her sister was doing in town on a Saturday morning.

Completely at home in Kate's apartment, Sky took a mug from the cupboard and set it under the spout of the coffee maker, then selected a coffee pod and dropped it into the machine. "Is he here?" she asked.

"Is who here?" Kate wondered.

Her sister grinned. "Sheriff Hottie."

She shook her head. "No. Of course he's not here."

"I don't know if I'm relieved or disappointed," her sister admitted.

"Relieved," Kate decided for her.

"There are times when I wish I could be more like you—every aspect of my life ordered and compartmentalized," Sky said. "But there are other times that I worry because your life is so ordered and compartmentalized."

Maybe that had been true before, but her impulsive actions in Boulder City had changed everything. "It's too early in the morning for deep philosophical musings," she protested.

"You need a guy who will shake up your life."

Reid Davidson had undeniably done that, but she still felt compelled to take issue with her sister's phraseology. "I don't need a guy at all."

"You're right." Sky nodded in acknowledgment even as her lips curved. "But you want him."

Since her sister would see right through any effort to deny it, she didn't even try. "Only because I always want what isn't good for me—like Sweet Caroline's caramel fudge brownie cheesecake."

"Mmm," Sky agreed, stirring sugar into her mug. "And why isn't that good for you?"

Kate breathed in deeply, as if the scent of her sister's coffee might be enough to jolt her sluggish brain. "Because one little slice has about a gazillion calories."

"Calories you could burn off with Sheriff Hottie," Sky suggested, taking a seat at the island.

Kate just shook her head. "Not going to happen."

Not again.

Of course, she hadn't intended for it to happen last night, either, but something happened whenever Reid touched her. A hormonal surge that short-circuited her brain, making her body spark like a live wire, humming and crackling with the electricity zipping through it.

She reached into the bread bag, retrieved two slices and slid them into the toaster, focusing intently on the task so she didn't have to look at her sister. Because just the memory of Reid's touch caused her blood to heat and pulse in her veins, and she could feel the warmth spread into her cheeks. "Do you want toast?"

"No, thanks, I ate at home. Martina made huevos rancheros this morning," she said, referring to the Circle G's longtime housekeeper.

"Lucky you." Though just the thought of eggs and chorizo sausage smothered in spicy salsa was enough to make Kate's stomach pitch.

"So," Sky said, when she realized her sister was watching her bread crisp, "are you going to explain to me what that whole 'I'm going to marry your sister' thing was about?"

Kate reached into the cupboard for a plate as the toast popped up. "It was clearly the rambling of a drunk man."

Sky seemed to consider the explanation as she sipped her coffee. "I can believe that alcohol was a factor in causing him to blurt out the declaration, but I suspect he had a reason to be hearing wedding bells. Which leads me to believe that either the new sheriff doesn't always live in the land of sane people or he's the guy you got naked with at that conference in Boulder City."

One of the best things about having a sister was that she could tell her anything. One of the worst things about having a sister was that she told her—and her best friend, Emerson—everything. And they forgot nothing.

"He's the guy I got naked with in Boulder City," she admitted, nibbling on the edge of a piece of toast.

And last night.

But there was no way she was going to share *that* information. It was one thing to confide that she'd had earth-moving sex with a guy her sister didn't know and was never expected to meet, and something entirely different to admit she'd done the deed with the man who was the new sheriff in town.

"And he immediately fell so head over heels in love with you that he decided to apply for Jed Traynor's job so that he could convince you to marry him?" Sky suggested dubiously.

"No. He applied for the position before we met. And I didn't know he was the new sheriff until I went to his office yesterday to discuss a case."

"How's Aiden doing?" Sky asked, proving that Kate's efforts to honor her client's confidentiality were for naught in a town where everyone knew everyone else's business.

"You know I can't talk to you about a client—or even confirm the identity of a client."

"You don't need to confirm it—his dad was overheard talking to Glenn Davis at the hardware store, and he said that you're the reason his son isn't stuck in a jail cell this weekend."

She sighed. "How am I supposed to maintain solicitor-client privilege if my clients—or clients' parents—don't keep their own mouths shut?"

"Okay, I won't ask any more questions about Aiden," Sky promised. "Which brings us back to the new sheriff, his proposal and your baby."

Kate sucked in a breath, then sputtered and coughed on the toast crumbs lodged in her throat.

Sky started to rise, but Kate held up a hand—holding her sister off—and swallowed a mouthful of lukewarm tea.

"Are you okay?" Sky asked.

She cleared her throat and nodded. "Yeah, you just... Where did that that idea about a baby come from?"

"It comes from knowing you, Kate. You're not drinking coffee, you're nibbling on dry toast—and you look like you're having trouble even keeping that down. Not to mention that most guys don't propose after a single weekend with a woman, so I figured Sheriff Hottie had to have a pretty good reason for doing so."

"Okay, you're right," she finally acknowledged. "I'm pregnant."

"You're going to be a mom," Sky said quietly, almost reverently. Then she grinned. "And I'm going to be an auntie." She hopped off her seat and embraced her sister. "I'm going to be the best auntie in the world—I promise."

"You can start by not telling anyone else about my pregnancy," Kate told her.

"I won't tell anyone," Sky assured her. "But how long do you think you can keep it a secret?"

"I don't know, but I just found out myself last week," she admitted.

"And told the sheriff last night—before he wandered into Diggers'," her sister guessed.

She nodded.

"Are you going to say yes?"

"He didn't actually ask me to marry him, Sky."

"But he will."

"How can you possibly know something like that?" Kate challenged.

"I study human behavior," Sky reminded her. "And the new sheriff is the type of man who truly believes it's his duty to serve and protect, and that sense of responsibility extends not just to the residents of his town but even more so to the people he cares about. He's honorable, upstanding and just traditional enough to believe that marrying the mother of his child is the right thing to do."

"No one rushes to the altar because of an unplanned pregnancy in this day and age," Kate reasoned.

"I'm going to offer you a piece of advice, anyway."

"What's that?" she asked warily.

"If you decide to marry him, let Dad walk you down

the aisle—don't run off to Vegas like Caleb and Brielle did," Sky cautioned.

Their brother's impulsive and short-lived marriage was rarely discussed—and never within earshot of their father.

"Dad wasn't mad that they went to Vegas to get married—he was furious that his son had knocked up a Blake." Although technically Brielle was a Channing, her mother was a Blake, which meant, for all intents and purposes, she was a Blake, too—and, therefore, an enemy of the Gilmores.

"But I promise that I won't run off to Vegas to get married," Kate said to her sister now. "Because I have no intention of getting married."

"Maybe you don't," Sky acknowledged. "But I wouldn't bet against Sheriff Hottie on anything."

Reid wanted to respect Katelyn's request for space, but considering that she'd asked for time before he'd left her apartment Friday night—and before they'd gotten naked together again—he figured that action wiped the slate clean.

Recalling her grandmother's mention of Saturday appointments, he tried her office first.

He walked in just as Katelyn was escorting a client to the door. There was no one else waiting in the reception area and the desk that he assumed belonged to a secretary or assistant was vacant.

Still, she didn't acknowledge him until her client had gone. "Did we have a meeting scheduled, Sheriff Davidson?"

"Nothing definite, Lawyer Gilmore."

She smiled at that, just a little.

He held up the manila envelope in his hand. "I have the discovery documents in the Johansen case for you."

She frowned as she took the envelope and lifted the flap.

"The Johansen case?" She pulled out the sheaf of blank papers, then looked at him.

He shrugged. "I figured I should have a pretext to justify my presence at your office."

"Very clever," she said.

"Was that your last appointment?" he asked.

"It was," she confirmed.

"Do you want to grab some lunch?"

"I appreciate the invitation," she said. "But I thought you were going to take some time to think about the situation."

"I've done nothing else since you told me that you're having my baby," he said.

"Why are you suddenly so willing to believe the baby's yours?"

"I wasn't disbelieving so much as stunned," he told her. "When you invited me to your place for dinner, the last thing I expected was for you to say that you were pregnant. And we weren't careless. I've *never* been careless."

"Neither have I," she said.

"I guess it's true that condoms are only ninety-eight percent effective."

"I could have lived a happy and fulfilling life without ever being proof of that statistic."

"And yet, here we are," he said.

"Here we are," she agreed. "And while I appreciate your willingness to charge full speed ahead, I'm not sure the revelation of my pregnancy has fully registered. I only told you about the baby—" she glanced at the watch on her wrist, did a quick mental calculation "—eighteen hours ago, and you were drunk for several of those."

His lips curved in a slow smile as his gaze skimmed over her. "We both know I wasn't drunk last night, Katelyn."

She turned away from him and slid the "documents" he'd given her into the paper tray of the printer beside the reception desk.

"But you're right," he acknowledged. "I didn't take the news well at first. On the other hand, it was the first time a woman's ever told me that she was going to have my baby, so I'm sorry I didn't know the right thing to say or do."

"It was the first time I've ever told a man he was the father of my child, so I might not have handled it the best way, either."

"But when I woke up this morning—alone and naked," he said, with another pointed look at her, "I was resolved."

"Resolved?" she echoed warily.

"To do the right thing."

She shook her head. "We can't get married, Reid—we hardly know each other."

"Living together as husband and wife will change that quickly enough," he told her.

She huffed out a breath. "I told you about the baby because I thought you had a right to know, but I don't want anything from you. As far as I'm concerned, no one else ever needs to know you're the father."

"Which proves your point that we don't know each other," he said. "Because if you knew me, you'd know that I'm not going to walk away from my child—or the child's mother."

Kate lowered herself into Beth's chair and pressed her fingers to her temples, as if that might alleviate the pounding inside her head. She hadn't expected that it would be easy to tell Reid about her pregnancy. She'd been prepared for him to question the paternity of her baby, and she'd expected that he'd need some time to accept the truth of what she was saying. She hadn't been prepared for him to jump from questioning to acceptance in the blink of an eye—and she hadn't expected him to jump from acceptance to marriage at all.

She felt his hands come down on her shoulders, and she jumped.

"Relax, Katelyn," he said, and began to massage gently.

It was easy for him to say—not so easy for her to do. He'd called her skittish the night before, and she couldn't disagree. She was certainly excitable whenever he was near.

And when he touched her, as he was touching her now, she melted. Which was precisely why she shouldn't let him touch her.

But she couldn't bring herself to ask him to stop. She didn't want him to stop. She wanted—

She abruptly severed the thought, unwilling to acknowledge her latent erotic desires.

"I know this isn't what either of us planned, but we're in it together now," he said, as he continued to loosen her muscles.

She wanted to believe it was true. Since the doctor confirmed her pregnancy, she'd felt alone and overwhelmed.

But it wasn't just her baby, it was his baby, too. And if he really wanted to be a *we*, there was part of her that couldn't help but think it would be easier than *me*.

But co-parenting suggested a level of relationship she wasn't ready for, and marriage was several levels beyond that.

"Why aren't you running away as far and fast as you can?" she wondered aloud.

"Because I don't shirk my responsibilities."

She turned the chair so that she was facing him, forcing his hands to drop away. "If you were one of my clients, I'd tell you to demand a paternity test."

"Why would I do that when you told me there's zero chance anyone else could be the father?" he asked.

"Because you shouldn't take my word for it," she protested. "I could be manipulating you for financial gain—or attempting to finagle a marriage proposal."

"I do have some savings and investments, which I'd willingly give to support our child, and I've already suggested marriage, but you're resistant to the idea."

She shook her head. "Do you have no sense of self-preservation?"

"Maybe I haven't known you very long," he acknowledged. "And there are undoubtedly a lot of things I don't know about you, but I know you're not lying about the paternity of the baby you're carrying."

"You seem to be handling the news a lot better than I did," she admitted.

"Believe me, I'm in full-scale panic mode on the inside," he told her.

"I'm familiar with panic. Although when I realized I was late, my initial reaction was denial. Because there are a lot of different things that can mess up a woman's cycle, and whatever had messed up mine, it couldn't possibly be a baby.

"But then a few days turned into a week, then two weeks. So when I was in Elko for a custody hearing, I went to a pharmacy to buy a home pregnancy test."

"It was positive?" he guessed.

She nodded. "But I still didn't believe it. I was sure that the test must have been faulty, or I'd somehow done it wrong."

"There's a wrong way to pee on a stick?"

She managed a smile. "It was easier to believe that than trust the result. So I bought a second test, but it was faulty, too."

"I'm sensing a pattern."

"I just couldn't wrap my head around the possibility that there was a tiny life growing inside of me," she admitted. "Maybe I'd always thought I'd be a mother someday, but someday was supposed to be a lot of years down the road."

"Then you bought a third test?"

"From a different pharmacy, because clearly the entire shipment at the first store was defective. When that test gave me the same result, I finally went to see Dr. Amaro."

"Have you told anyone else?"

She shook her head. "My sister knows, but I didn't tell her. In fact, it was your mention of marriage that tipped her off."

"I was thinking out loud," he admitted.

"Believe me, I know what a shock it is to discover that, after a casual hookup, you're going to be a parent."

"I never would have said, 'Hey, let's have unprotected sex and see what happens,'" he acknowledged, "but the reality of a baby changes everything."

She instinctively touched a hand to her belly. "The reality is only about the size of a lentil right now."

"A lentil? Is that like a bean?"

"Close enough," she said.

"That's pretty small."

She nodded. "But he or she will do a lot of growing over the next seven months."

"Still, a little bean would benefit from having both a mom and a dad looking out for him or her, don't you think?"

Chapter Eight

Kate had never understood why expectant parents referred to an unborn child by cute nicknames, but she couldn't deny there was something about the way Reid said *little bean* that was endearing. She also appreciated that he'd used both gender pronouns rather than defaulting to the masculine as so many people—especially men—tended to do.

Except that, despite his warm tone and conciliatory demeanor, he was doing exactly what Sky had warned her he would do—trying to push her toward marriage so that he could feel better about doing "the right thing."

Thankfully, she knew how to push back.

"Reid, I only found out about the baby a few days before you did, and I'm not ready to think about all the ways my life is going to change. I know it's going to change," she acknowledged, "but getting married is definitely not a change that ever crossed my mind."

"Think about it now," he suggested.

She sighed. "Don't you already have one divorce behind you?"

"Yeah," he admitted.

"So why would you want to rush into another marriage, especially one that would be doomed from the start?"

"Why do you think our marriage would be doomed?"

"Because we'd only be getting married for the sake of our baby," she pointed out to him.

"I can't think of a better reason."

"What about love?" she challenged.

"Is that what you're holding out for?"

"I'm not holding out for anything," she denied. "But whenever I thought about getting married, I assumed it would happen because I was in love with the man I was planning to spend my life with."

"I'm sorry this situation is forcing you to deviate from your plan," he said. "But I'm not going to pretend to be in love with you so you can feel better about marrying me."

"I don't want you to pretend anything, and I don't want to marry you," she told him.

Except that she did want to give her baby a real family—the kind that she'd known for the first twelve years of her life. Since the death of her mother, a crucial piece of their family had been missing, and Kate couldn't help but worry that her child might feel the same emptiness growing up without a full-time father.

"But I appreciate your willingness to do the right thing," she said to Reid now. "Even if we're not in agreement as to what that is."

"Your pregnancy is one of those curveballs life likes to throw at us to see how we'll respond," he told her. "I'm ready to step up to the plate and hit that ball out of the park."

She rolled her eyes. "I'm guessing you're a baseball fan."

"My Rangers tickets were the only thing I was sorry to leave in Texas," he admitted.

"Just one more thing I didn't know about you—because I don't know you," she said again.

"Just one of the many things we have yet to discover about one another," he countered, putting a different spin on the point.

"Well, there's something you should know about me," she told him. "I hate the Rangers."

He winced. "Despite that blasphemous statement, I'm willing to trust that your failure to appreciate America's pastime isn't indicative of greater character flaws."

"I don't hate baseball," she said, eager to clarify her previous statement. "I hate the Rangers because I'm an Angels fan."

"Now that might be indicative of greater character flaws," he said, shaking his head sadly.

"You won't find many Rangers fans in Nevada, and in this part of the state, they're mostly Dodgers or Athletics fans with a handful of Angels and Giants supporters in the mix."

"How'd you end up cheering for the Angels?"

"Three years at UCLA," she reminded him.

"Okay, let's put aside our differences with respect to baseball for the moment and focus on what's best for our baby."

Our baby.

The words spilled out of his mouth easily, as if they didn't twist his stomach into painful knots. And maybe they didn't. Maybe he'd accepted the reality of their situation a lot more easily than Kate had done, because as much as she loved her unborn child already, there were moments when her doubts and fears seemed stronger than anything else.

Her biggest concerns were based on not knowing how she would manage to juggle her career and the demands of a child. And, of course, long before the baby was born, she was going to have to tell her father about her pregnancy.

He'd be supportive, but he'd also be disappointed to learn she would be a mother before she was a wife. And he'd probably wonder if the death of her own mother so many years earlier had somehow caused her to fall into bed with a man she barely knew.

A ring on her finger would reassure her father that, although she'd made a mistake, she'd be taken care of. Because while David Gilmore was open-minded enough to encourage his daughters to be anything they wanted to be, he was also old-fashioned enough to believe a woman needed a man to take care of her.

Yes, as difficult as it would be to tell him she was pregnant, she knew he'd accept the news more easily if it was followed by *and I'm going to marry the father of my baby*.

But she wasn't going to take what looked like the easy path now, because it would only be that much harder later on when the relationship fell apart and their child was caught in the middle of a messy divorce.

"Can we please just take some time before making any life-altering decisions?" she asked him now.

"How much time do you think you need?"

"Eight months?" she suggested, aware that their baby would be born before that period of time had passed.

He folded his arms over his chest and looked at her as if she was a recalcitrant child. Maybe he was practicing his stern father facade and, if so, he was doing a good job—which made her want to both laugh and cry, because her emotions were a complete mess.

"More than a day," she told him.

"Okay," he relented.

"And, in the meantime, can we keep this...news...between us?"

"I'm already an outsider—and not in any hurry to face the judgment that will follow when people find out I got Katelyn Gilmore pregnant."

"I'm willing to keep the paternity of my baby a secret," she reminded him.

But Reid shook his head stubbornly. "I'm not."

He gave her a week.

And every day that passed during that week, he waited for his phone to ring or for Katelyn to show up at his office. But it never happened, and Reid was beginning to suspect that it never would.

So he took the initiative—and a pizza—and crossed his fingers that she wouldn't toss the box back in his face when he showed up at her door.

After buzzing him in, she eyed him with suspicion—and the pizza box with interest. "What are you doing here, Reid?"

"Well, you made dinner for me last week, so I figured it was my turn," he explained. "But I'm not much of a cook, so this seemed like a safer option."

"What's on the pizza?"

"Pepperoni, black olives and hot peppers."

"Since it would be too much of a coincidence to discover that those are your favorite toppings, I'm guessing you asked my sister what I like."

"Guilty."

With a sigh of resignation, she stepped away from the door so he could enter.

He could tell she was wary, so he deliberately kept the

conversation focused on neutral topics while they ate, and they chatted about local news, current events and baseball scores of their rival teams. They didn't discuss Aiden Hampton, although Reid knew that she'd talked to the ADA about a local diversion program that would allow Aiden to take responsibility for his actions and perform community service in exchange for a withdrawal of the charges.

"Let's go to a movie," he suggested, when the pizza box was empty.

"Why?"

"Because it's Friday night and there's nothing good on TV."

"I have a brief to research and write."

"Come on, Katelyn—it's Friday night. Play hooky with me."

She bent down to scoop up a napkin that had fallen onto the floor. "There are only two screens at the local theater— it's quite possible there's nothing good at the movies, either."

"You can choose between the latest Marvel movie and some artsy-sounding film that I've never heard of," he told her, making it clear what his choice would be.

She grinned. "Who doesn't love superheroes in spandex?"

They found seats inside the theater, then Reid went to get snacks while Katelyn thumbed through the messages on her phone, just so that she had something to focus her eyes on while her mind wandered. She wished she'd had the opportunity to get to know Reid better without the specter of her pregnancy hanging over them. But, of course, the tiny life growing inside her changed everything. Even if no one else knew about the baby right now, there would be speculation about the relationship—and more so when her condition became evident.

Reid came back carrying a tray with two soft drinks, a big bag of popcorn, a package of licorice and box of Milk Duds.

"If I didn't know otherwise, I'd think you'd skipped dinner," she commented.

"Those aren't for me." He put the drinks in their respective cup holders, then set the tray of snacks in her lap. "They're for you."

"For me?"

"I didn't know what you liked."

"I like everything," she admitted, keeping her voice quiet to ensure that no one seated around them would overhear their conversation. "But I'm not actually eating for two, you know."

"Then you could share with me," he suggested.

"Hmm…that was your plan all along, wasn't it?"

He winked as he settled into the seat beside her. "Maybe."

It was almost like a real date, and it made Kate wonder how things might have played out if a condom hadn't failed. How would she have responded to discovering that he was the new sheriff of Haven?

She would have been pleased to see him. Because even before she'd begun to suspect that there were consequences of her trip to Boulder City, she hadn't stopped thinking about those two blissful nights. But she also would have been wary of any kind of personal relationship, because he was now wearing a badge in the town where she was building her law practice. It wasn't a direct conflict of interest, but Kate would have wanted to steer clear of the slightest appearance of impropriety.

Of course, being pregnant with the new sheriff's baby

took away that option. And even if no one else knew the truth about their relationship, being seen with him at the local movie theater would generate a fair amount of talk. And maybe, since Reid was prepared to acknowledge paternity of the baby, she was subconsciously hoping that people wouldn't later count the number of weeks between his arrival in town and the arrival of her baby and realize she was pregnant before he showed up in Haven.

The lights in the theater dimmed, and she settled deeper into her seat to focus on the coming attractions. But if she'd hoped the movie might provide a distraction from thinking about her pregnancy, she hadn't anticipated that sitting beside Reid in the dark theater distracted her from everything else. Everything but her awareness of the man.

An awareness that intensified with every brush of his leg and every bump of his arm. And when he leaned close to whisper in her ear, the scent of him—clean, simple and masculine—tempted her more than the buttery popcorn.

Determined to ignore the hunger stirring in her veins, she tore open the box of Milk Duds and popped a chocolate-coated caramel into her mouth, letting it sit on her tongue until it began to melt. And she continued to pop candy into her mouth, one at a time, until the box was empty.

"Licorice?" Reid offered the bag to her.

She shook her head. "No, thanks."

Because she'd already consumed an overload of sugar and it had done nothing to curb her appetite for what she really wanted but couldn't have.

He set the licorice and the half-empty bag of popcorn aside and reached for her hand, linking their fingers together. At first, she felt self-conscious and wondered if the overture was intended as some kind of statement about their relationship. But the theater was dark, making it unlikely that anyone could see their hands.

So they watched the rest of the movie like that, their fingers entwined in the dark. And when she stopped trying to read any deeper meaning into the gesture, she could admit that it felt surprisingly nice.

But she also suspected this was part of his campaign to convince her to do "the right thing," and she wasn't convinced that marriage was the right thing.

She knew that relationships didn't come with guarantees, but getting married because of an unplanned pregnancy seemed like a guarantee of heartache. And yet, she was tempted to accept his offer, because heartache at some distant time in the future seemed preferable to the doubts and insecurities about being a single mother that plagued her now.

Of course, the characters in the movie were battling much bigger problems, so she put aside her own thoughts and concerns and let herself be drawn into the action on the screen.

When the credits began to roll and spectators started to exit the theater, Reid gave her hand a subtle squeeze and released it, preserving the illusion that they were acquaintances simply enjoying a movie together. It was a perfectly legitimate and believable explanation for them being together, but Kate decided that if people were going to talk, she might as well give them something to talk about.

She led the way out of the theater and, after dropping her empty Milk Duds box and drink cup into the garbage, reached for his hand again.

"Thank you," she said, as they exited onto the sidewalk and the crowd began to disperse in various directions.

"For what?"

"For tonight—the pizza, the movie, the snacks. But especially for helping me forget about everything for a couple of hours."

"It was my pleasure," he told her.

"You might feel differently when you're fielding questions from everyone who saw us together tonight."

"There were questions before we hit the ticket counter," he confided.

"From who?" she asked.

"Jolene Landry," he said, naming the owner of Jo's Pizza. "Apparently the pepperoni, hot peppers and black olives combo is known to be your particular favorite."

"I didn't think about that," she admitted.

"Well, Jolene now believes—at least, I think I managed to convince her—that those are my favorite toppings, too."

"But the pizza combined with being seen together at the movie is going to be grist for the gossip mill."

"There is one way we could nip it in the bud," he said.

"What's that?"

"We could announce our engagement."

She sighed. "I should have known you couldn't let it go for ten minutes."

"I let it go for more than three hours," he countered. "But I'll make you a deal."

"What kind of deal?" she asked warily.

"I'll stop bringing up the subject if you promise to give serious consideration to the idea and let me know when you've made up your mind."

"I have made up my mind," she told him.

"*Serious* consideration," he said again.

"Okay," she relented, withdrawing her keys from her pocket as they approached her building.

"Promise?"

"I promise." She unlocked the door. "Good night, Reid."

He held the door. "I'll see you up."

"It's really not necessary," she protested.

"It is," he insisted. "Unless you want me to kiss you good-night right here, where we're illuminated under the security light for anyone who might be passing by."

"Maybe I don't want you to kiss me good-night." Of course, she did, but kissing Reid tended to lead to other intimacies, and she was determined to ignore the sexual attraction between them. Or at least try.

"I still want to see you safely inside," he told her.

Because she suspected it was true, she let him follow her up the stairs to the second floor, where she unlocked the interior door to her apartment and turned on the lights.

He did a quick visual scan of the open area, as if to be sure that everything was as they'd left it, then moved to the windows, checked that the latches were all fastened, and nodded.

"Do you want to look for monsters under my bed, too?" she asked.

"Lead the way."

She shook her head. "I'm *not* showing you my bedroom."

His lips curved in a slow and blatantly sensual smile. "Well, the sofa worked just fine at my place."

She didn't need the reminder. She remembered, in very clear and vivid detail, every kiss and touch they'd shared that night—and the two nights they'd spent together in Boulder City. And that was why it was a bad idea to let him touch her again.

"We have to be smart about this," she told him. "We have to think not just about what we want but what's best for our baby."

"What's best for our baby is to have two parents who are together."

"That's not always true," she said. Being a family law

attorney, she'd had a front-row seat to the drama that ensued when marriages—and families—fell apart, and she had no desire to add a failed union of her own to the statistics.

"You're right," he admitted. "But I know we could make it work, because we're both too stubborn to accept anything less than success—and because the sizzling chemistry between us would go a long way toward smoothing any bumps in the road."

"Just like a guy to think that sex is the answer to everything."

"Not everything," he denied. "But—"

Whatever else he'd intended to say was cut off by the abrupt ring of his cell phone.

Reid cursed under his breath as he pulled the device out of his pocket and glanced at the screen.

"Aren't you going to answer that?" she asked, when he made no move to do so.

"I'd rather not," he admitted.

"It's almost midnight, and no one calls at midnight unless it's important." She lifted her brows as another thought occurred to her. "Or a booty call."

"It's not a booty call," he assured her.

But he touched the keypad to connect the call, and Kate wandered into the kitchen to give him some privacy.

"Sorry about that," Reid said, after he'd finished with the call and tucked his phone away again.

"Was it something urgent?" she asked.

"Everything's urgent to Trish."

"Trish?" she queried, before she could stop herself.

"My ex-wife," he told her. "She called to tell me that she's in labor."

Chapter Nine

Reid didn't think about how his words might be interpreted until Katelyn's eyes went wide.

"You're going to be a father?"

"What? *No!*" His emphatic response was followed by a short laugh. "Well, yes, but only to your baby."

Her brow furrowed, as if she couldn't make sense of what he was saying. "Your ex-wife is having another man's baby?"

"Yes," he confirmed.

"You don't seem too upset by that," she noted.

"Why would I be? The other man's her husband."

"Her husband?"

"We've been divorced for four years," he explained. "And Trish has been remarried for three of those."

She opened her mouth to speak, then closed it again without saying a word.

"You're wondering why she called to tell me about a baby that isn't mine?" he guessed.

"Maybe. Yeah," she admitted.

"Because my ex-wife has no concept of boundaries."

She considered his response before asking, "How long were you married?"

"Two-and-a-half years. But we were friends for a long time before we got married, and we continued to be friends after our marriage fell apart."

"That's...surprising."

"And possibly a mistake," he acknowledged. "I can't imagine ever completely cutting ties with her, but I recently accepted that those ties were a little too close, which is one of the reasons I decided to move away from Echo Ridge."

"And ended up in Haven—having to deal with another woman who's going to have a baby," she noted.

He nodded.

"You know, it's probably not too late for you to get out," she said. "Isn't there a probationary period during which you can decide that the job isn't working out—or that Haven isn't what you were looking for?"

"Whether or not any of this is what I wanted, it's what we've got," he said.

And though the idea of fatherhood was no less terrifying now than when he'd first learned of her pregnancy, he remained committed to doing the right thing. He just had to convince Katelyn to let him.

"Well, if you're determined to stick around, I have a favor to ask," she said.

"Anything," he immediately replied.

"You might want to wait until you know what I want," she suggested.

"Anything," he said again.

"I'd like you to come with me to the Circle G for a barbecue Sunday afternoon."

"You want me to meet your family?"

"You've already met my grandmother and my sister," she reminded him. "But yes, I'd like to introduce you to everyone else, too, so that when I get around to telling them I'm pregnant, they will have met the baby's father."

He was surprised by the invitation, because he suspected that showing up at the ranch with Katelyn would create a lot more speculation than going to a movie in town. But he only asked, "What time should I pick you up?"

After Kate closed the office door behind her last client Saturday afternoon, she sent a quick text to Emerson Kellner—her best friend since kindergarten. Kate had been the maid of honor when Emerson got married three years earlier, and the godmother of her first child at Keegan's baptism six months ago.

Her message, asking if Emerson was up for some company, received an immediate reply: YES! PLEASE!

Aware of her friend's fondness for white chocolate macadamia nut cookies, Kate stopped at Sweet Caroline's Sweets on the way and picked up a dozen of the treats.

"I'm still carrying eight pounds of baby fat," Emerson protested, eyeing the white bakery box in her friend's hands.

"You look fabulous," Kate told her sincerely. "But it's really my godson I want to see."

She'd first held the baby only a few hours after his birth. He'd had wispy blond hair, a pert little nose, a rosebud mouth and tiny hands curled into tiny fists. And when he'd opened his eyes, she'd fallen head over heels in love. Ten months later, she loved him even more.

"He'll be waking up from his nap soon," Emerson promised, moving toward the back of the house. "In the meantime, I've got a pitcher of lemonade out by the pool, where you can tell me about the sexy new sheriff."

Kate stretched out in the lounger beside her friend. "Why are you asking me about him?"

"Because I heard you had a date with him last night."

"I did not," she denied.

"Really?" Emerson said skeptically. "Because Lacey Bolton heard from Deanna Nardone that Megan Carmichael saw you snuggled up with an—" she made air quotes with her fingers "—'unknown hottie' at the movies last night."

"I hate this town," Kate muttered, tipping her head back and closing her eyes.

"Were you at the movies or not?"

"Yes," she admitted.

"And?" her friend prompted.

"It's definitely worth the price of a ticket. If you and Mark want to see it, I'd be happy to watch Keegan."

"I wasn't asking about the movie," her friend chided. "And don't think I didn't notice your failure to comment, positively or negatively, on my description of the sheriff as sexy, which suggests to me—and remember, I know you better than anyone else—that he's got you all churned up inside."

He did, of course, although not only for the reasons her friend was thinking. "His name is Reid Davidson and yes, he's tall, dark and handsome."

Emerson shook her head. "No skimping on details."

"Approximately six-two, short brown hair, hazel eyes, strong jaw, broad shoulders."

"You've always had a thing for guys with great shoulders," her friend noted.

"Is that description adequate?"

"It's helping me put together a mental picture," Emerson confirmed. "But I need a number."

"Seriously, Em, we're not in high school anymore."

"I know. I'm an old married woman stuck at home with a baby now—I need to get my thrills vicariously."

"You're twenty-eight years old, married to the love of your life and Keegan is the most adorable baby in the world."

"It's all true," she admitted. "But I still want a number."

The number system they'd established in high school for rating the guys they liked was hardly unique. Emerson had never dated anyone who was less than an eight-point-five and Kate had never dated anyone at all.

After watching *Erin Brockovich* with her mother, Kate had announced that she was going to be a lawyer someday. Her mother had been both proud and supportive of her goal, and when Tessa died, Kate had been more determined than ever to follow through with her plan. And while her best friend was dating all the cute boys at their high school, Kate was focused on getting into college and then law school. She had no intention of letting any guy—even a ten-plus—derail her plans.

"Assigning a number is insensitive and objectifying," she protested.

"He's a ten-plus, isn't he?" Emerson guessed.

Kate answered with reluctant honesty. "Yeah, he's a ten-plus."

"And they're in short supply in this town," her friend noted. "You better snap him up before someone else does."

"I'm at the building-my-career phase of my life," she said, conveniently ignoring—at least for the minute—that she was also at the growing-a-life phase way ahead of schedule.

"Things don't always go according to plan," Emerson

warned. "You can't predict when you'll meet the right guy and you shouldn't pretend he isn't the right guy just because the timing is wrong."

"But if it's the wrong time, is he really the right guy?" Kate countered, attempting to divert her friend's focus.

"Would you sleep with him?" Emerson pressed, proving the effort ineffective.

She hesitated, just a fraction of a second, before responding, "Actually...I already did."

"Oh. My. God. I should have realized...when you mentioned the shoulders—he's the sheriff you knocked boots with in Boulder City."

Kate rolled her eyes. "Yes, he's the one."

"You told me the sex was spectacular," her friend recalled. "Off-the-charts spectacular, in fact."

"With the proviso that I'd been celibate for a long time prior to that weekend, so my assessment might have been a little bit skewed."

"And now he's Haven's new sheriff." Emerson picked up her lemonade, sipped. "Was that a coincidence or is he stalking you?"

"Coincidence," Kate assured her. "He actually interviewed for Jed's job before the conference started."

"Maybe fate then," her friend suggested.

"Please don't make this into something that it isn't. And please don't tell anyone—even Mark—that I hooked up with Haven's new sheriff."

"I can't lie to my husband," Emerson protested.

"You won't have to lie because it's not going to come up in conversation if you don't bring it up," she said, lifting her hand to cover a yawn.

"Fine—but it's not like he'd tell anyone else."

"Too many people know already."

"Who else knows besides me, you and the sheriff?"

"My sister," Kate confided.

"You told Sky before you told me?"

Admitting that Reid had told Sky—more or less—would create more questions, so she only said, "I saw Sky before I saw you."

"Still." Emerson pretended to pout. "I'm your best friend. I'm supposed to hear all the important stuff first."

"You were the first person I told when I came back from Boulder City," she said soothingly.

That revelation didn't appease her friend, who was studying her through narrowed eyes. "You're still holding something back."

Thankfully, before Emerson could press her further, a cheery babble sounded through the baby monitor on the table.

Kate immediately pushed herself up off the lounger. "Keegan's awake."

"Awake but not fussing," her friend noted.

"That's my favorite kind of baby," she said, opening the sliding door.

"Wait until you have one of your own," Emerson warned, following her into the house. "Believe me, after the first few months of constant demands, you won't be in such a hurry to pick him up every time he makes a sound."

Which was going to happen a lot sooner than her friend suspected—and a lot sooner than Kate ever would have predicted. But now that she'd had a couple weeks to get used to the idea, she could confidently say that the prospect of impending motherhood filled her with more joy than trepidation. She still had fears and concerns, but the happiness that filled her heart when she thought about holding her baby in her arms was so all encompassing, it managed to hold those fears and concerns at bay.

Or it had until today when a client's child-from-hell had

screamed like a banshee for the whole forty minutes she was in Kate's office.

She followed the familiar path up the stairs and down the hall to the nursery, peeking in to see that Keegan had pulled himself up on the bars and was gnawing on the rail, drool dripping off his chin.

He looked up and grinned when he recognized his godmother.

"Oh, my goodness," Kate said. "Look at all those teeth."

He smiled again, showing them off.

"Aren't you such a big boy now?"

He released his grip on the rail and lifted his arms toward her, a silent request to be picked up. But without the support of the rail, he lost his balance and immediately fell down onto his bottom. His little brow furrowed.

"Oopsie daisy," she said, and he giggled. She reached into the crib and lifted him out. "Kiss?"

He puckered up and touched his lips to her cheek.

"A little sloppy, Keeg," she said. "Hopefully you'll fix that before adolescence." She patted a hand against his bottom. "And give some consideration to potty training, too."

"Do you want me to change him?" Emerson offered.

"I can handle a wet diaper," Kate assured her.

Emerson settled into the rocking chair in the corner of the room, content to let her friend handle the diaper duties. "Remember—he's a boy."

Kate nodded. The first time she'd ever changed Keegan, she hadn't thought to cover him when she pulled the wet diaper away and he'd sprinkled like a fountain. "I don't think I'll ever forget."

Clean diapers and wipes were within easy reach, and she had everything ready before she unsnapped the fasteners of his romper. He immediately twisted, trying to roll away from her.

"Get over here, Mr. Wiggly Worm," she chastised, splaying her hand across his belly to hold him in position.

"He certainly is that," Emerson agreed. "I remember how thrilled I was when he finally rolled over at five months—now I just wish he would hold still every once in a while."

"My grandmother says that new parents spend the first year of a child's life eager for him to walk and talk—and the next sixteen wishing he'd sit down and shut up."

Emerson laughed. "I'm sure there's some truth in that."

When Keegan tried to roll over again, Kate reached for one of his favorite teething toys. She jingled the plastic keys, immediately snagging his attention. He kicked his chubby legs and stretched his arms out for the toy.

She jingled the keys again, then let him take them from her so she could secure the tabs of his diaper and fasten the snaps of his romper. When that was done, she dropped the dirty diaper into the bin beside the table and picked up the baby, propping him against her hip.

"I've figured it out," Emerson said, when they were once again reclining in the loungers by the pool, Keegan sitting in Kate's lap. "What you've been holding back."

The baby tossed the keys to the ground, and Kate reached to scoop them up—a familiar game between them. "What do you think I've been holding back?"

"You're pregnant."

This time the plastic keys slipped out of *her* hand.

"I'll take that as a yes," Emerson said, retrieving the toy for her son.

It wasn't just the words but the absolute conviction in her friend's voice that warned Kate any effort to deny the truth would be in vain. And maybe she'd come here for this—to talk to somebody who knew her better than anyone else and who knew what it meant to be a mother.

"Am I wearing a sign?" she wondered aloud, a little un-nerved that first her sister and now her best friend had so readily uncovered her secret.

Emerson smiled. "There are all kinds of signs if some-one knows you—especially if that someone has recent ex-perience with pregnancy."

"What kind of signs?"

"You're pale and fatigued and your boobs are practi-cally spilling out of your bra."

Kate's gaze immediately dropped to her chest. "Ap-parently you know me even better than I realized," she remarked.

"But does *he* know?" Emerson asked.

She nodded.

"How'd he respond?"

"He thinks we should get married."

Her friend's brows lifted. "What do you think?"

"I don't think a broken condom is the first stop on the road to wedded bliss." Kate rubbed Keegan's back. "If and when I get married, I want it to be because I've fallen in love. Maybe that's selfish under the circumstances, but I want what you and Mark have," she said, imploring Em-erson to understand.

"Anyone would have reservations in your situation," her friend acknowledged. "But you wouldn't be pregnant if you and the sheriff didn't have some powerful chemistry."

"And if that was a valid reason for a legal union, the tra-ditional wedding vows would forgo mention of love, honor and cherish in favor of lots of really hot sex."

"The love, honor and cherish stuff is easier to do when there's lots of really hot sex added to the mix," Emerson said.

Which wasn't all that different from the argument Reid had made but still didn't hold much sway for Kate.

"I had a client—a young, single mom—come in today with a six-month-old. She wants an order to compel a DNA test so she can get financial support from the baby's father. She also said she wouldn't mind if Dad wanted to take the baby off her hands some of the time.

"Which seemed an odd comment to me, at first," Kate noted. "Until the baby, suddenly and inexplicably, started screaming. The mom checked her diaper, offered a drink and a snack, but nothing soothed the kid. The baby kept screaming until even the mom was crying, and…I'm terrified that's going to be me in the future."

"I've been there," Emerson confided. "There are times when it seems nothing I do will soothe Keegan, then I start to doubt everything I'm doing and feel like a total failure as a mother.

"I can only imagine how much harder it would be if I didn't have Mark to help out, so if you came here for reassurance, I'm not sure I can give it," her friend said. "Don't get me wrong—I love Keegan with my whole heart and I love being a mom, but there are days I'm so overwhelmed, I don't realize until Mark gets home that it's dinnertime and the breakfast and lunch dishes are still in the sink because I haven't had a chance to empty the dishwasher. And I'm still in my pajamas because I didn't have time to get dressed—or even notice that I wasn't.

"It's even worse when Mark's out of town on business. Last week, he was gone for three days. When he finally got back, as soon as he walked through the front door, I handed him the baby and walked out. I just needed some space, just five minutes by myself, so that I could hear myself think."

"Thanks," Kate said drily. "I feel so much better now."

"I wouldn't be a true friend if I told you it was all smiles and giggles," Emerson said. "Although those smiles and giggles do have a way of making you forget about poopy diapers and projectile vomit—at least in the moment.

"Still, I know how much you've always wanted a real family of your own," her friend continued in a gentler tone. "So before you make any final decisions, you need to consider all your options—including saying 'I do' to the sexy sheriff."

Chapter Ten

Katelyn wanted to be at the Circle G around four o'clock. Reid had mapped the route on his phone and discovered it was about a thirty-minute drive from her apartment, so he was at her door promptly at 3:30.

She was ready when he arrived and immediately came out rather than buzzing him in. She was wearing a sleeveless white V-neck top printed with tiny blue flowers over a pair of slim-fitting navy capri pants with white leather slip-on sandals. Her hair tumbled in loose waves over her shoulders, the ends dancing in the light summer breeze.

She looked cool and casual and far too sexy for his peace of mind. Certainly no one looking at her would ever suspect that she was pregnant.

"Boy or girl?" Katelyn asked, fastening her seat belt.

"Huh?" he said.

She smiled as she slid a pair of dark sunglasses over her eyes. "I assume your ex-wife had the baby by now—I was wondering if it was a boy or a girl."

"Oh. Yes, she did. A boy," he told her. "Henry."

"Are you hoping our baby is a boy or a girl?" she asked.

He pulled out of the parking lot and turned onto Page Street. "I can't honestly say that I've given the matter any thought."

"Think about it now," she suggested.

Thinking about her pregnancy was scary enough without imagining the baby that would come at the end. Reid didn't have a lot of experience with kids, but he knew infants were completely dependent on their parents for everything—food, clothing, shelter, attention and affection.

"Or is it too soon to be thinking about the sex?" she wondered.

"I'm always ready to think about sex," he told her.

A smile tugged at her lips as she shook her head. "I meant the sex of our baby."

"Oh. Yeah, it's too soon to be thinking about that," he agreed.

Definitely too soon.

He wasn't ready to be a father, and he didn't imagine himself being any more ready in seven months.

Maybe seven years.

Yes, that might work.

Or, better yet—never.

Unfortunately, that wasn't really an option.

"I've thought about it," she admitted. "I don't have a preference, but it's fun to imagine what our son or daughter will look like."

He considered for a moment, then shook his head. "I don't want to imagine what our daughter would look like."

"Why not?"

"Because now I'm picturing her with dark hair and

blue eyes like her mom, so breathtakingly beautiful that my badge and gun will be my only hope of keeping the boys at a distance."

"And then she'll sneak off for a weekend, somewhere away from the watchful eye of her overprotective father, and get knocked up," Katelyn warned.

He slid her a look. "Not *my* daughter."

"I'm sure that's what my father would have said, too," she agreed. "If anyone had suggested the possibility to him."

His fingers tightened on the steering wheel. "He's going to want to kill me, isn't he?"

"Wanting and doing are completely different things," she said, as if to reassure him. "And I'm not planning to tell him today."

"What are you going to tell him?" Reid wondered. "Will you be introducing me as the new sheriff or your boyfriend?"

The way she nibbled on her bottom lip before responding suggested that she hadn't considered any of the details. "I guess it wouldn't hurt to give them the impression that we're dating," she admitted. "It would certainly make it easier to explain a baby later on—but no PDAs."

"What about sneaking up to the hayloft?" he asked, only half teasing.

"That would be another no," she said firmly.

He wasn't surprised by her response, but he was disappointed. "Anything else I should know before I meet your family?"

"Just don't mention the name Blake and everything should be fine."

"Are the Gilmores and the Blakes still feuding?"

"The Hatfields and McCoys of Nevada," she told him.

"I'll have to remember not to get on your bad side," he mused. "Apparently Gilmores know how to hold a grudge."

"Only as well as Blakes," she retorted.

"And all because one guy got the prime land and the other ended up with some precious metals."

"Wars have been fought over less," she remarked. "And then there was the ill-fated love affair between Everett Gilmore's daughter, Maggie, and Samuel Blake's youngest son, James."

"I haven't heard that part of the story," he admitted.

"It's not unlike so many other forbidden love stories. Boy meets girl, their families disapprove, they run away together. Then the families come together, at least temporarily, to track down their missing offspring and drag them home again."

"Something must have happened to widen the rift again after that," Reid guessed.

She nodded. "Eight months later, Maggie died pushing her stillborn son into the world and James, overwhelmed by grief and guilt, set off on horseback and was never seen again. That story has been retold to each successive generation of Gilmores—and probably Blakes, too—as a warning of the kind of tragedy that results whenever the families forget that they're enemies."

"Just don't tell it to the little bean as a bedtime story," Reid suggested. "It's kind of dark."

"It is," she agreed. "And yet, my brother Caleb managed to forget the ending for a while."

"He fell in love with the daughter of your father's archenemy?" he guessed.

"I don't know if he loved her," she said. "But for a few weeks, he was married to her."

"Now that sounds like an interesting story."

"It's not even a unique one. They were young, they

screwed around, Brielle got pregnant and Caleb took her to Las Vegas for a quickie wedding. She lost the baby, they got a quickie divorce—end of story."

"Really?" he said dubiously. "That's it?"

"That's it," she confirmed. "After that, Brielle went away to school in New York City, and I don't think she's been back more than once or twice since."

"Maybe she's still in love with your brother," he suggested.

"Or maybe she's happy in New York," she countered.

"What about your brother—is he happy?"

"He's never given any indication that he's not," she said. "Liam, on the other hand, makes no secret of the fact that he has ambitions other than waking up at the Circle G every morning for the rest of his life."

"What does he want to do?"

"Renovate the old Stagecoach Inn and reopen it as a boutique hotel and spa."

"That doesn't sound like a bad idea," he said. "Aside from the Dusty Boots Motel out by the highway, Haven doesn't have a hotel."

"I don't disagree that a hotel is a good idea—if somebody else wanted to tackle the project, but 'Gilmores are ranchers,'" she said, deepening her voice in what was clearly intended as an imitation of her father.

"Did he object when you decided to go to law school?"

She shook her head. "My dad might have strong opinions about—well, he has strong opinions about everything," she acknowledged. "But he appreciates that everyone, even ranchers, need lawyers."

Reid turned where she indicated, passing through the open gates under an arched metalwork sign announcing Circle G Ranch.

The paved highway gave way to a gravel road and

stones kicked up under his tires, pinging against the un-dercarriage. He trusted that she knew how to get to the ranch, but the road he was on seemed to go nowhere. Every direction he looked, there was nothing but open fields dotted with cattle and, in the distance, the Silver Ridge Mountains speared into the cloudless blue sky. It was a full three minutes after he'd pulled off the highway before the house—two impressive stories of timber frame and cut stone—came into view.

He parked his truck, noting that there were five pick-ups, three SUVs and two ATVs ahead of his vehicle in the driveway.

"Good," Katelyn said, already reaching for the handle of her door. "It looks like everyone's here."

"You told me that you had a sister and two brothers," he reminded her, as he unhooked his belt.

"That's right," she confirmed, exiting the truck.

He followed suit, albeit less eagerly. "So who do all these vehicles belong to?"

She laughed at the obvious trepidation in his tone. "The gray truck is my dad's, the red one belongs to my grand-parents, the pimped-up Jeep is Caleb's, Liam usually drives the green truck and Sky the blue SUV. The others belong to my uncle and cousins and the ranch foreman."

"This is a usual family dinner?"

"Pretty much," she confirmed, then nudged him with her shoulder. "Come on—I'll introduce you."

She did so, and though she'd given Reid a brief heads-up with respect to everyone else in attendance, it was appar-ent that Katelyn's family had received no advance warn-ing that she'd be bringing a date.

"Trust me," she said later, when they moved toward the paddock to check out the foal born a few days earlier. "It's better that they didn't know you were coming, because they didn't have a chance to prepare an interrogation."

"Thank you, I think." Then, as he looked around the property, he had to admit, "This place is impressive."

"Six generations of Gilmores have worked to make it a success."

"It must have been quite an experience to grow up here, surrounded by all of this."

"It was," she agreed.

"And a big adjustment—moving from one of the biggest ranches in Haven to an apartment in town."

"It was," she said again.

"You don't miss this?"

She shook her head. "I miss my family sometimes, although it seems as if someone always has an excuse to make a trip into town to check up on me, but I don't miss the ranch."

There was something in her voice, a hint of defiance that he suspected was a deliberate cover of a deeper pain.

"You didn't grow up wanting to be a cowgirl?"

"No," she said. "Not since I was twelve, anyway."

"What happened when you were twelve?"

She was quiet for a moment. "My mom died."

He winced. "I'm sorry, Katelyn."

She just nodded and continued walking. After a few minutes, she stopped beneath a Jeffrey pine, her gaze fixed somewhere in the distance. "My mom loved everything about the ranch," she told him. "And she worked as hard as any of the hands. But sometimes, early in the mornings, she would saddle up her favorite horse and just ride. And sometimes she'd let me go with her. I loved those early morning rides when it was just the two of us."

Reid could see where the story was going now and regretted that he'd asked.

"We were out by the eastern border near the creek that morning. I saw something moving on the ground, but before I could say anything, Honey spotted it, too, and instinctively reared up. My mom was a good rider—skilled and experienced—but she'd been pointing to something in the distance and was unprepared for the abrupt movement.

"She was thrown off the back of the horse," she continued, her voice flat now and all the more heartbreaking for the lack of emotion in it. "And broke her neck when she fell.

"I didn't know what to do," Kate admitted. "She probably had a cell phone, but I didn't think about that at the time. Instead, I raced back to the house, to get help. My dad called 911, then he went after her. By the time he got to her, it was too late."

"I'm so sorry," Reid said.

"I didn't ride for a long time after that," she confided, as they made their way back to the paddock. "I hated Honey, I hated all the horses and the chores and everything about the ranch.

"I don't hate it anymore, but I don't think I'll ever love it the way I used to."

"Losing someone you love has a way of changing things," he acknowledged, reflecting briefly on his abandonment by his mother, his grandmother's death, and then the loss of Hank, too. Each of those events had played a part in making him the man that he was today—and his determination to be a father to the baby Katelyn was carrying.

"I miss her every single day, but now…now that I'm going to be a mother myself, the wound is somehow fresher and deeper again," she told him.

"I didn't tell anyone, when I first suspected that I might be pregnant, but I would have told her. I'm not saying she would have been overjoyed to hear that her unmarried daughter was having a stranger's baby, but she would have listened without judging…and she would have loved our baby."

He slid an arm across her shoulders and drew her to his side, a silent gesture of support. She let her head fall against his shoulder, for just a minute before she said, "Is this a PDA?"

"Nope—there's no one else around, so it's strictly a DA."

She laughed softly. "You know, under other circumstances, I could really like you, Sheriff."

"Why can't you like me under current circumstances?"

"Because current circumstances are complicated."

"Life is complicated."

"And although we're having a simple meal tonight, I should see if Martina and Grams need a hand in the kitchen."

"Very smooth segue, counselor."

She responded with a sassy smile. "Do you want to come back to the house with me?"

"I'll hang out here for a while," he decided.

Ten minutes later, when he was flanked by her brothers and cousins, he was wishing he'd opted to return to the house with Katelyn.

"Are you on duty or off?" Caleb asked, offering a beer to him.

"Off," he said, nodding his thanks as he accepted the bottle.

"I have to make a trip into town later and I wouldn't want to run afoul of the law," Liam said, explaining the soda can in his hand.

"Heather again?" One of the cousins—Mitchell—asked.

Liam grinned. "Yep."

"This is going on what—three weeks now?" the other

cousin—Michael—asked. "That's a long-term relationship for you."

"As much as I enjoy roasting my brother," Caleb interjected. "We're getting sidetracked from the real issue here."

And they all turned, as if on cue, to look at Reid.

He tipped the bottle to his lips, sipped. "Am I an issue?"

"That's what we're trying to figure out," Caleb told him.

"Katie doesn't usually bring a date to family events," Liam commented.

"Katie doesn't *ever* bring a date to family events," Mitchell clarified.

"Then I'm doubly honored to have been invited," Reid said.

"Of course, as a defense attorney, she'd understand the importance of establishing a positive relationship with local law enforcement," Liam noted.

"Which might be why she included you," Caleb suggested.

"I know better than to question a woman's motives," Reid told them.

"We want to know if the two of you are dating," Michael said, cutting to the chase.

"I'm enjoying spending time with her," he said, since he wasn't sure that one date actually qualified as dating.

"You can't have spent much time with her yet," Liam said. "You've only been in town a few weeks."

"Actually, I knew Katelyn before I moved to Haven."

The brothers and cousins exchanged a look, clearly not pleased by this revelation.

"From where and for how long?" Caleb asked.

"From 'none of your business' and as long as 'none of your business,'" Katelyn responded from behind them.

The five men turned to face her.

"You're our sister," Liam reminded her.

"And our cousin," Mitchell piped in.

"That makes it our business," Caleb finished.

"While I acknowledge and appreciate that the name carries a certain weight and status in this town, being born a Gilmore doesn't automatically imply the forfeiture of any expectation of privacy."

Michael slanted a look at Caleb. "Now you've done it."

"When she's really annoyed, she starts with the lawyer-speak," Liam explained to Reid. "And since I've got horses to feed before dinner, I'm going to go do that before she really gets on a roll."

"We'll help you," Michael said.

They all moved away from the paddock together.

Kate folded her arms and leaned them on the rail, her gaze fixed on the foal that was prancing on spindly legs beside its mother.

"I'm sorry," she said. "I knew my family would have questions when we showed up together, but I thought they'd exercise some discretion."

"They're just looking out for you," he noted.

"Maybe," she allowed. "Although sometimes I think they harass people just for sport."

"They did seem to have a good rhythm going with their interrogation, as if they'd had a lot of practice."

"No doubt they have," she agreed, then hastened to clarify. "Interrogating Skylar's numerous boyfriends in high school, I mean."

"What about your boyfriends?"

She shook her head. "I didn't date in high school."

"Not much or not at all?"

"Not at all," she admitted. "I was more interested in studying than boys."

"So when did you have your first boyfriend?" he asked.

"My first year of college, but even he didn't get an invitation home to meet my family."

"Who was the first guy who did?"

"I, uh…actually, I can't remember."

His gaze narrowed. "You remember—you just don't want to tell me."

"It's really not important," she told him.

"Your refusal to share the name suggests otherwise."

She sighed. "If I tell you, you're going to wish you'd let this go," she warned.

"Maybe," he acknowledged. "But I still want to know."

"You," she said.

He waited for her to finish her thought, but that single word was all she said.

"What about me?" he prompted.

"You, Sheriff Reid Davidson, recent transplant from Echo Ridge, Texas, are the first man I've ever brought home to meet my family."

She had to be joking. There was no way he was the first. Except that the flags of color high on her cheeks gave credence to her claim.

"How old are you?" he blurted out.

She laughed. "Twenty-eight." Then, after a tiny hesitation, she added, "Today."

And the surprises kept coming. "It's your birthday today?"

She nodded.

"Happy Birthday."

"Thanks."

His mind was still reeling over the first revelation—that she'd never introduced a man to her family. She must have had boyfriends—because she wasn't a virgin when they were together. But he was beginning to realize he'd misjudged her experience. "So what happened between us in Boulder City…"

"My first ever one-night stand," she admitted.

"And not technically a one-night stand."

She nodded.

"I turned thirty-four in March," he told her.

"Happy belated birthday?"

He managed a smile. "I just wanted you to know that there's a six-year age gap between us."

"Does that bother you?"

"Are you kidding? Guys always want to be with hot young chicks."

She laughed. "Is that what I am—a hot young chick?"

"Very hot—and younger than I realized," he admitted.

"But we're not really together," she reminded him.

"Are you sure? Because I'd guess your family is thinking that we're not only together but that our relationship is pretty serious, since I'm the first guy you've ever brought home to meet them."

"You know why I wanted them to meet you."

"So it doesn't come as a shock when you tell them we're getting married?" he asked hopefully.

Chapter Eleven

Kate shook her head, exasperated by his unwillingness to give up on the idea—and increasingly tempted to take what he was offering. But for the moment, she held firm. "We're *not* getting married."

"I haven't stopped thinking about you since the weekend we spent together in Boulder City," he told her.

"I'm flattered," she said. "But that's no reason to start planning a wedding."

"You're right," he agreed. "But what about a baby? Do you think having a baby is a good reason?"

"I'd say it depends on the preexisting relationship between the expectant parents," she said. "If there was no preexisting relationship, then I'd have to say no—a baby is not a good reason to get married."

"What if those two people, despite having no preexisting relationship, somehow just click whenever they're together?"

"I'm not sure 'click' is either a valid or relevant factor," she said dubiously.

"It's both," he insisted.

"Sometimes an attraction just confuses the issue," she pointed out.

"I'll admit to being confused about a lot of things, but wanting to marry you isn't one of them."

And when he said it like that, with unwavering conviction, she almost believed it was true. But she knew he didn't really *want* to marry her, he just wanted to do the right thing. And she definitely didn't want to have the same arguments with him again.

"We should get back," she said instead. "Dinner will be ready soon."

It was almost dark by the time they'd said their goodbyes to everyone and drove away from the ranch. Though Reid knew her family still had a lot of questions about his relationship with Katelyn, he considered the afternoon a success. Of course, everything would likely change when they found out she was pregnant, so he was grateful she didn't seem to be in a hurry to share that news.

"Your family sure knows how to put on a barbecue," he commented, fondly recalling the platters of ribs and burgers and sausages, heaping bowls of potato salad, coleslaw and macaroni and cheese, the enormous pot filled with homemade baked beans and baskets with thick slices of corn bread. It had seemed like a mountain of food, but the mountain was soon conquered by the Gilmores and their guests.

"My family doesn't believe in doing anything by half measures," she told him.

"I enjoyed meeting them," he said as he turned onto

the highway to head back into town. "Thank you for inviting me today."

"I'm glad you survived," she said, a smile playing at the corners of her mouth. "I know they can be a little... overwhelming at times."

A little overwhelming was something of an understatement. On the other hand, he'd enjoyed watching Katelyn with her relatives—the teasing and shorthand communications that develop through close relationships. The way one person would start a story only to have someone else pick up the narrative of the shared experience without missing a beat.

"You were lucky to grow up in such a close family."

"I know," she acknowledged. "Even if I didn't always think so at the time."

He'd been on his own for so long, he'd forgotten what it meant to be connected to someone else. Being with Katelyn's family today had given him a glimpse, and he was glad their baby was going to be part of that family.

"I realized something else today," she told him.

"What's that?" he asked.

"That you don't talk about your family."

"There's not much to talk about," he said. "For a long time, it was just me and my grandmother. Then I spent some time in foster care, living with other people's families, until Hank took me in."

"Who's Hank?"

"Hank Mahoney was the Sheriff of Echo Ridge when I was growing up there."

"He's the reason you went into law enforcement?" she guessed. "To follow in the footsteps of a man you admired?"

"Yeah," he admitted. "Although it was a little more complicated than that."

"It's a long drive back to town," she reminded him.

She was right, and even if there were parts of his history that he wasn't proud of, she deserved to know his background.

"I first met Hank when I was seventeen," he told her. "Young and dumb enough to attempt to hot-wire the sheriff's truck."

Her brows lifted. "You can really do that? I thought that was just something that happened in the movies."

"I can really do it, but I'm not very good at it—which is why Hank caught me in the act. I'd just been bumped from yet another foster home and, thankfully, he recognized that I was acting out of anger and frustration more than I was looking for trouble, and he gave me a chance."

"Like you did with Aiden, once you knew the whole story."

He kept his gaze focused on the road. "What makes you think I did anything?"

"Haven't you learned yet that it's next to impossible to keep a secret in Haven?" she chided. "When I went to see the ADA about the charges against Aiden, he said Rebecca Blake had already called to tell him that, after consultation with the new sheriff, she supported Aiden's application for the youth diversion program."

"Not a lot of people know about the program," he said, as if that was his only reason for reaching out to Mrs. Blake. "And Aiden's a good candidate, with a father determined to keep him on the straight and narrow."

"How old were you when you lost your parents?" she asked gently.

"I didn't lose them—they lost me," he told her. "My dad was a drunk who took off before I was born. Apparently he came back again, around my first birthday, but didn't hang around for more than a few months. My mom stuck it out for a few more years, hooking up with the occasional boyfriend who made my dad look like a catch. Then when I was about six, she decided that taking care of a kid was too much responsibility and dumped me at her mother's house.

"I don't know what excuse or explanation she offered, but my grandmother took me in and, for the next eight years, she raised me. Then she died, and I had no one.

"I bounced around in foster care for a while, because teen boys don't tend to settle easily into traditional families, and I spent some time in a group home, where I started to run with a bad crowd and made some poor choices."

"Like hot-wiring the sheriff's truck."

He nodded. "I know it sounds melodramatic, but I really believe he saved my life that day."

"Did Hank have any kids of his own?"

"A daughter, Patricia. She was a year ahead of me in school—the cheerleader who dated the quarterback." He lifted a hand to rub the slight bump on the bridge of his nose. "One night when I was leaving school late, I saw them together. They were in the middle of a pretty heavy makeout session and I wanted to look away, but something about the situation set off warning bells in my head.

"Long story short—she was saying no, he wasn't listening, so I intervened. He punched me in the face, broke my nose, Trish helped me mop up the blood and drove me home."

There was something different in his voice when he said her name, an unexpected warmth that made Kate wish she'd never asked.

She definitely shouldn't ask the next question that sprang to mind, but there was a time delay between her brain and her mouth and the words spilled out before she could stop them. "You fell in love with her?"

"No," he denied. "But I married her."

He'd been upfront about his divorce from the beginning, but he hadn't mentioned that his wife was the daughter of a man who'd been his father figure, mentor and best friend.

And again, though she wasn't sure she wanted all the details, she heard herself ask, "How did that come about?"

"Hank got cancer," he said bluntly. "When he realized he was dying, his biggest concern was his daughter. He didn't want to leave her alone, without anyone to look out for her. I told him that I would and put a ring on her finger to prove it.

"I wasn't in love with her," he said again. "But it wasn't just a quick ceremony to appease her dad, either. When I spoke my vows, I intended to honor them forever."

Kate knew that marriage required a leap of faith, regardless of the reasons for it. She also knew there were all kinds of reasons that marriages—even good marriages—fell apart, and she couldn't deny a certain curiosity about his. "What went wrong?"

"We wanted different things," he said.

"That's rather vague," she noted.

"There were issues that drove us apart and no compelling reason to stay together."

His follow-up response didn't do much to expand on the first, but she decided to let it go. No doubt it was, if not painful, at least uncomfortable to talk about a failed marriage. And now that she knew some of Reid's background, she could understand and appreciate why he was so determined to be there for their baby.

Childhood wounds inevitably left a mark, and although she hadn't been so young when she'd lost her mother, the sense of loss and emptiness was still with Kate every single day. She suspected that Reid's experiences had left even deeper scars and that his determination to be there for his child was a way of ensuring his son or daughter had a better start in life than he'd been given.

Katelyn was quiet for a long while after Reid told her about his upbringing, probably questioning his suitability as a parent. He didn't blame her for having doubts—he had more than a few of his own. But a few days earlier, he'd heard her argue a case that made him believe she'd give him a chance.

Her client was a father seeking to alter a custody order. If Reid remembered the details correctly, the dad had worked long hours in the mines and wasn't much of a hands-on parent for the first few years of the children's lives. Now he was a manager, with a more regular schedule and weekends off, and wanted increased access to his children. The mother balked at the request because she was in a new relationship and the children were settled into routines that she didn't want to disrupt.

Listening to the lawyers, Reid couldn't help but wonder if he and Katelyn would someday end up in front of a judge, arguing about who was entitled to what with respect to their child. He didn't want their son or daughter to become a pawn in a game of one-upmanship, but he would fight to be part of the child's life.

For now, though, he continued to hope that wouldn't be necessary. There was still time to convince Katelyn to marry him and give their baby a real family, but he understood her reservations. She was in court almost every day dealing with the aftermath of marriages that didn't work—contentious divorces, property disputes, custody fights. Even if they'd fallen in love after dating a while, she'd undoubtedly have reservations about making any lifelong promises—and he didn't know how to overcome those reservations.

How could he claim to know anything about making a marriage work when he'd already failed to do exactly that? Of course, the circumstances of his first marriage were completely different. Hank had been dying and Reid would have done anything to ease the man's worry in those final days.

He hadn't been in love with Trish and he hadn't pretended that he was. And even though she'd claimed to love him, he suspected the feelings she professed to have were born of a fear of being alone. She wanted to love and be loved, and when Reid couldn't give her what she wanted, she found someone who could.

It was ironic that one of the reasons his marriage had fallen apart was that his wife wanted a baby and he didn't. Now, by accident rather than design, he was going to be a father, anyway. The role he'd been certain he didn't ever want was suddenly his.

More surprising was the realization that he *wanted* to be a father to the baby Katelyn was carrying. In fact, he was starting to accept that he wanted to be a father *and* a husband—he wanted them to be a family. But first, he had to convince Katelyn that it was what she wanted, too.

"Did the judge make a decision in that custody variation hearing you had last week?"

"You were in the courtroom?"

He nodded.

"Since when does local law enforcement take an interest in a standard family law matter?"

"I only popped in to check out the hot young lawyer at first," he admitted. "But your arguments were compelling and, afterward, I found myself wondering if you believed them."

"You're going to have to be a little more specific," she told him.

"You said the variation wasn't about the dad's right to spend more time with his children but about their right to have a meaningful relationship with both parents."

"Wow, you were paying attention, weren't you?"

"The case struck a chord," he admitted.

"Yes, I believe it," she said. "It's important for a child to be given the opportunity to develop a strong and lasting bond with both parents."

"What does that mean for us?"

Her brow furrowed as she turned to stare out the window. "I would accommodate whatever reasonable visitation you wanted."

"I don't want visitation," he told her. "I want to marry you and raise our child together."

"We don't have to be married to co-parent our child," she assured him.

"I don't want our child to be co-parented," he argued. "I want him—or her—to have a real family. And I think you want that, too, you're just afraid to admit it."

"Of course it's what I'd want if our situation was different—if our baby had been conceived in the course of something that actually resembled a relationship rather than as a consequence of a broken condom during a one-night stand."

"Two nights," he reminded her.

"A second night doesn't miraculously turn a casual hookup into a relationship."

"And an unplanned pregnancy shouldn't be used as a roadblock to the development of a relationship," he argued.

"Especially not when there are so many other obvious roadblocks," she agreed.

He turned onto Station Street. "Why'd you go to Echo Ridge looking for me?"

She gave up the pretense that she'd been in Texas for any other purpose. "Because you're the father of my baby."

He nodded. "Now let's consider for a minute what might have happened if I hadn't already agreed to take over Jed Traynor's job here in Haven."

"You would have been in Echo Ridge," she acknowledged, not sure where this new train of thought was leading.

"Most likely," he agreed, making the turn onto Main. "And you would have tracked me down at the Sheriff's Office and told me about our baby, right?"

She hesitated, but she couldn't deny the truth of what he was saying or see how that truth would trip her up. "Right," she confirmed.

"Even though we'd gone our separate ways and you could have kept the news of your pregnancy to yourself."

"You're the father of my baby," she said again. "And fathers have specific legal rights and responsibilities."

He nodded and turned onto Page, then into the parking lot behind her building. "And when you told me about your pregnancy, you gave me the opportunity to exercise those rights and fulfill the responsibilities."

"Because it was the right thing to do."

"And maybe," he suggested, "because there was a part of you that wanted me to step up, not just to be a father but a husband."

Kate thought about his supposition for a long time after Reid had gone. Her initial instinct had been to deny it, of course, but there was some validity to his argument.

She believed that a child had a right to a relationship with both parents; she didn't believe that a child's mother and father had to be married to parent effectively. Maybe marriage would make some things easier, but that was hardly a reason to get trapped into a legally binding arrangement.

Except that the more time she spent with the sheriff, the less the prospect of marriage seemed like a trap. In fact, the idea of marrying Reid was starting to hold some definite appeal.

Chapter Twelve

Two weeks later, Reid had made little progress in his efforts to convince Katelyn to marry him. For every step he took forward, she took two steps back. Sometimes it was a struggle to even get her to spend time with him. She seemed to have a ready excuse whenever he called to make plans, but she was less inclined to turn him down face-to-face. He took that knowledge with him to her door early Friday night.

"If you keep hanging around my apartment, people are going to start to talk," Katelyn warned, but she stepped away from the door so that he could enter.

"I've got nothing to hide." He followed her into the living room, stopping abruptly when he spotted the playpen in the corner, an assortment of colorful blocks scattered across the area rug and a blond-haired, blue-eyed, chubby-cheeked baby wearing an orange T-shirt and brown overalls with a giraffe embroidered on the front.

The baby was sitting upright and gnawing on a purple block, but he glanced up at Reid and grinned, showing off tiny teeth. "Da!"

"Was I in a coma for—" he looked at the baby, estimated his age and added that to the time remaining in Katelyn's pregnancy "—eighteen months?"

"Ha ha." She scooped the baby up from the floor and propped him on her hip. "That's not Daddy, that's Sheriff Davidson."

"Da!" he said again.

"Don't worry," Katelyn said. "He thinks every man is 'Da.'"

"And who is he?" Reid asked.

"This is Keegan," she told him. "My godson. I'm babysitting for a few hours while Emerson—his mom and my best friend—has an appointment at the spa."

"Haven has a spa?"

"Well, right now Andria has a modest setup in her basement, but she's in negotiations with Liam to move her business to the hotel when it opens."

Keegan stuck his thumb in his mouth and dropped his head to Katelyn's shoulder, snuggling in comfortably. Seeing her with the baby in her arms, Reid felt something move inside him—an unexpected warmth that seemed to start in the vicinity of his chest and spread outward.

He'd spent a lot of time reading up on pregnancy and trying to prepare for the baby that would arrive in another six-and-a-half months, but he really didn't know what it took to be a father. Watching Katelyn with Keegan, he was reassured that their child would at least have one competent parent.

"You're a natural," he noted.

"He's an easy baby," she said.

His brows lifted. "Is there such a thing?"

"Well, most of the time he's an easy baby," she amended, as the little guy twisted in her arms to reach toward the blocks on the floor. "He did give me some trouble a few months back when he was teething, but once those pearly whites broke through, he was a smiling—and drooling—baby again."

"How old is he?"

She set Keegan down again, and he immediately grabbed the purple block. "Ten-and-a-half months."

"So we've got a while to wait before our baby will be teething and crawling?"

"And opening cupboards and trying to stick toy keys in electrical outlets."

He noticed that her outlets were protected with plastic inserts. There were also clear rubber bumpers affixed to the sharp edges of the coffee table. "Do you babysit often?"

"I try to take him for a few hours every couple of weeks, sometimes just to give Emerson a break, sometimes so that she and her husband, Mark, can have some time alone together."

"You're a good friend."

"Thank you," she said. "Emerson claims I borrow her baby to pretend I have a life outside of work."

"I guess you don't get out much."

"You've been in Haven long enough now to know there's really nowhere to go."

"Maybe that's why I always end up at your door."

She smiled at that. "Why are you really here?"

"Because I was thinking about you, and while I was thinking about you, I realized I was hungry, so I decided to see if you wanted to grab a bite and catch a movie."

"Dinner and a movie—that sounds a lot like a date, Sheriff."

"Maybe, if you had to put a label on it," he acknowledged. "Or it could just be a couple of friends-slash-colleagues hanging out."

"I appreciate the invitation," she said. "But Emerson is picking up pizza and wings on her way back."

"Maybe just the movie later, then?" he asked hopefully.

"Mark's out of town this weekend so we're having a girls' night—no boys allowed."

"What about him?" Reid asked, jerking his head toward the baby, who'd traded in the purple block for a green one.

"He gets a pass because his boy parts are in a diaper."

He sighed regretfully. "Okay, I guess I'll head over to Jo's and get my own pizza to take home and eat by myself."

She led him back to the foyer, a clear signal that his attempt to elicit sympathy and procure an invitation had failed.

But when she opened the door, he found himself face-to-face with a slender woman with curly reddish hair and a stack of three flat boxes in her hand.

"Well, hello, there," she said, her green eyes sparking with curiosity. "You must be Reid."

"I am," he confirmed, stepping back so that she could enter.

"And Reid was just leaving," Katelyn said.

"Oh," her friend said, sounding disappointed. "Have you had dinner?"

"I'm going to pick up a pizza on my way home," he said.

"Why would you do that when we've got plenty of pizza—and wings—right here?"

Keegan, having recognized his mother's voice, abandoned his blocks and crawled to the foyer, where he was now attempting to pull himself up on her leg.

"There's my little man," she said, smiling down at the baby.

Katelyn took the boxes. "How much food did you get?"

Emerson lifted the baby, rubbing her nose against his and making him giggle, then propping him on her hip. "They had a special on two pizzas and wings."

"We're never going to eat all that," Katelyn said.

"Then I guess it's a good thing we've got the sheriff here to help," she said, winking at Reid.

"I was just on my way out," he reminded her, showing his willingness to accede to Katelyn's wishes.

"Don't go without having something to eat first," Emerson protested.

He looked at Katelyn, silently questioning.

"Fine—you can stay for a slice of pizza," she relented, handing the boxes to him. "I'll get plates and napkins."

"Can you hold Keegan for a sec while I grab drinks?" Emerson asked when he'd set the food on the table.

Before he could respond—which would have been to suggest that he'd get the drinks—she'd shoved the baby at him, leaving him with no choice in the matter.

He looked down at the little guy who was looking up at him, lower lip quivering. "Oh, crap. You're going to cry, aren't you?"

As if on cue, the baby's big blue eyes filled with tears.

"Hey, this wasn't my idea," he said, talking fast in the hope of distracting the kid long enough for his mom to return. "And I don't blame you for being unhappy with the situation, but your mom will be right back, she just went to help—I assume, since she's your godmother, you call her Aunt Katelyn, or maybe Aunt Katie—get drinks so that we can have dinner."

To his surprise and immense relief, the monologue seemed to do the trick. Though the tears didn't dry up, Keegan's lip was no longer quivering and he looked more curious than scared now.

Reid kept talking. "What do you like to drink with your

pizza? Is your beverage of choice milk or juice? And do you drink from a bottle or a sippy cup?"

Of course, Keegan didn't respond to any of the questions, but the little guy at least seemed to be listening.

So was Kate, who had paused in the doorway between the kitchen and the dining room, plates and napkins in hand.

"I'm running out of things to say now," Reid continued in the same easy tone. "But I'm afraid if I stop talking, you'll start crying and your aunt Katelyn will realize I don't have a clue when it comes to babies and then she'll worry I'm going to be a horrible father.

"And while I'll admit that's entirely possible—and probably understandable considering that I have no memories of my own father and didn't have any positive male role models in my life until I met Hank when I was seventeen—I'm going to do my best to be a good dad and hope like hell—

"Heck!" he quickly amended. "I mean heck. I'm going to hope like heck that I don't screw up too badly. I suspect swearing in front of a baby would probably count as a screwup, so maybe we can just keep that to ourselves?

"And maybe you could actually smile and pretend I'm incredibly amusing and entertaining, and maybe that'll help convince Katelyn to give me a chance—"

Kate felt an elbow in her ribs and glanced at Emerson, who was also observing the sheriff's interaction with her little boy.

"If you had to get knocked up, at least you picked a stand-up guy," Emerson noted in a whisper.

"You're making this assessment after overhearing two minutes of a one-sided conversation with an infant?"

"A conversation in which he demonstrated honesty, vulnerability, self-awareness and determination," Emerson noted. "All that, and those fabulous shoulders, too."

Of course, her friend was right. And the more time Kate spent with Reid, the more irresistible he seemed, which made her question why she was continuing to resist.

She pushed aside those tempting thoughts.

"Come on. Pizza's getting cold."

Keegan sat in his mother's lap, gnawing contentedly on a piece of crust while the adults chatted and ate. When everyone had their fill and Kate got up to wrap the leftovers, Emerson said, "Oh, my goodness—is it almost eight o'clock already? I need to get this little guy changed into his pj's and home to bed."

Then she hurried into the bedroom, where Kate had laid a protective sheet on top of her comforter as a makeshift change table for the baby. Kate, of course, followed.

"What are you talking about?" she demanded. "I thought we were going to hang out tonight."

"Except that I forgot the seventeen loads of dirty laundry waiting at home," her friend said as she stripped away Keegan's overalls and T-shirt.

Kate's eyes narrowed. "Oh, no, you don't."

"But I do," Emerson insisted, pulling a sleeper out of the diaper bag. "Soon enough you'll understand how many onesies and burp cloths a baby goes through in a week."

"I'm sure you do have laundry to wash," she acknowledged. "That's not what I'm referring to."

"What are you referring to?" Her friend expertly slid a clean diaper under Keegan's bottom before unfastening and whisking away the wet one.

Kate folded her arms over her chest. "You're taking off because you think that will push me and Reid to spend more time together."

"If you need to be pushed, you're not nearly as smart as I always thought you were," Emerson chided.

But apparently it wasn't enough to push Kate, because Emerson returned to the living room and said to Reid, "Have you got a ring yet? Because The Goldmine has a sale on diamond jewelry this weekend."

Kate sighed. "Emerson's been my best friend since kindergarten," she told him. "But she's never been subtle."

"I've never understood why anyone would tiptoe around an issue when the direct approach gets you to the same place so much faster," Emerson said.

He nodded in acknowledgment of the point before responding to her question. "I might be new in town, but I've been here long enough to know that buying a diamond at The Goldmine would be as discreet as putting an engagement announcement in the Haven Record."

"Sexy *and* smart," Emerson noted. "Okay, putting aside the question of a ring for the moment—what are your intentions with respect to my best friend?"

"You should be more concerned about my intentions," Kate interrupted. "Because right now, killing you seems to be the only way to shut you up."

Her friend just grinned, unrepentant. "You shouldn't issue death threats in front of the sheriff."

But Reid didn't seem to have any qualms about answering Emerson's original question, because he said, "My intention is to marry Katelyn so we can raise our child together."

"And I still maintain that we don't need to be married to raise our child together," she chimed in.

"Blah blah blah," Emerson said, clearly having heard it all before and not at all concerned about upsetting her friend.

"It's true," Kate insisted.

Emerson directed her next comment to Reid again. "All the time Katie spends in divorce court has made her wary of putting her heart on the line."

"Reid doesn't want my heart," she interjected. "He just wants his ring on my finger to legitimize his claim to our child."

He was stunned by her matter-of-fact tone as much as the words. "Is that what you really think?"

Katelyn shrugged, as if it didn't matter. "We both know you never would have proposed if I wasn't pregnant."

"I can't deny that's true, but I don't just want our baby to carry my name," he said. "I want him or her to have the love and support of both parents, not one or the other depending on where he or she's sleeping on any particular night."

"That's a pretty compelling argument," Emerson noted, as she buckled the sleepy baby into his car seat.

"I thought you were in a hurry to get home," Katelyn said to her.

Emerson hugged her friend. "I'm going," she promised. Then she hugged Reid, too. "Don't give up on her—she'll come around."

"I'm keeping my fingers crossed."

"You might have more luck if you put a diamond on hers instead."

Kate shook her head as she closed the door behind her friend. "I'm sorry about that."

"I'm not," he said. "I like her straightforwardness."

"That's one word for it," she agreed.

"And I'm hoping the direct approach will work for me, too," he said, reaching a hand into his pocket.

Her heart started to beat faster when she recognized what was clearly a jeweler's box, and she took an instinctive step back. "What are you doing?"

"I'm proposing, Katelyn."

"Why?"

"Because while I've frequently mentioned that I want us to be married, I've never actually asked you to be my wife."

"You really bought a ring?"

He flipped open the lid to reveal a stunning princess-cut diamond.

As she stared at the glittering stone, Kate wondered why the prospect of marrying a man she'd known only a few months was somehow less terrifying than the idea of having a baby on her own. That he wanted to marry her and be a father to their child told her a lot about the type of man he was, but even if he was willing to vow to "love, honor and cherish" her, she knew he didn't love her.

And she didn't love him.

The five words hadn't fully come together to form a sentence when her heart bumped against her ribs, as if to contradict her claim.

No, her head insisted. It wasn't possible that she'd fallen in love with Reid.

Was it?

She took a minute to review the evidence. Every time she was going to see him, she felt flutters of anticipation in her belly that she knew—only ten weeks into her pregnancy— couldn't be explained away as movements of the baby inside her. She enjoyed talking to him and even arguing with him, because he challenged her to consider different ideas and opinions. And there was no doubt she was attracted to him. Those little flutters were nothing compared to the way her pulse jolted whenever he gave her one of those lingering looks that said he was remembering her naked. Or the way her pulse would race when he touched her—even just a casual brush of a finger down her arm. And when he kissed her—

Ohmygod.

She *was* in love with him.

But her feelings were only one side of the equation. If and when she ever walked down the aisle, she wanted it to be with butterflies in her tummy and hope in her heart— and looking toward a groom whose eyes were filled with love as he looked back at her.

Reid was looking at her now, but all she could see in his eyes was a steely determination to do the right thing.

"Katelyn Gilmore, will you—"

"Stop!"

"You didn't let me finish the question," he said mildly.

"Because if you don't actually ask, then I don't have to say no and we can pretend this never happened."

He rose to his feet again but continued to hold the box open, the brilliant diamond flashing light. "There is another option, you know—you could say yes."

She shook her head regretfully, her throat tight. "I can't."

Then, because she didn't trust herself to hold back the tears that filled her eyes or the newly acknowledged feelings overflowing from her heart, she turned and walked briskly to her bedroom, closing the door firmly behind her.

Chapter Thirteen

She hadn't actually said no, but Reid knew that if he'd pressed the issue, she would have. Maybe they weren't head over heels in love, but he sincerely liked and respected Katelyn. And then there was the sizzling sexual chemistry between them…chemistry that she'd been determinedly ignoring, causing him to suffer through a lot of cold showers in recent weeks.

If she'd said yes to his proposal, one of the perks would be warm showers with his bride-to-be, sliding soapy hands over the sexy curves of her body. Unfortunately, his erotic fantasies seemed destined to remain just that.

If she was adamantly opposed to marrying him—and rushing away in tears didn't suggest that she was on the fence—he had to respect her choice. Even if he wasn't happy about it.

He didn't want to share custody of their child, with scheduled weekend trade-offs and formal discussions about homework or afterschool activities, but he was determined to be there for his son or daughter as much as possible. To be the full-time father he'd never had as a kid.

Still, he was frustrated with the whole situation, so when he stepped outside Saturday morning and saw Norm Clayton pressing one hand to his back while the other struggled with the cord of the lawn mower, he offered to take over. The old man protested at first—after all, the sheriff was paying rent, he shouldn't have to do chores—but Reid assured him that he didn't mind. So Norm retreated inside to his heating pad and Reid welcomed the roar of the mower drowning out thoughts of his aborted proposal.

The backyard required some maneuvering around the climbing structure and sandbox that Norm and Bev had installed for their grandchildren to enjoy when they visited, which got Reid thinking he was going to need a backyard for his son or daughter to run around in. Because he didn't plan on living in the Claytons' downstairs apartment forever and a child needed space.

And toys to scatter around the yard.

And maybe a dog.

He'd finished the cutting and was pushing the mower back toward the garage when he saw Katelyn on the sidewalk.

She smiled, a little tentatively, as she moved closer. "Moonlighting in yard work, Sheriff?"

"Norm's back was bothering him this morning, so I offered to help."

"Did you sell tickets?"

"What?"

"You have an audience," Katelyn noted, sliding a glance toward the neighbor's porch where Beverly Clayton and Frieda Zimmerman were sipping glasses of lemonade.

"They're not watching me," he denied.

"You don't think so?" She lifted a hand in greeting and both women immediately waved back.

"It's a real scorcher today, isn't it?" Beverly called out.

"It sure is," Reid agreed, wiping the sweat from his brow with his forearm.

"Eighty-seven degrees already," Frieda said. "And supposed to get hotter."

"There's an extra glass here," Beverly told him. "If you want some lemonade to help you cool off."

"Or you could just take off your shirt," Frieda suggested as an alternative.

"Frieda!" Beverly admonished.

"We're not out here to watch the clouds move across the sky," her friend and neighbor said bluntly. "We want to see the sheriff's muscles."

Katelyn bit down on her lip, obviously trying not to laugh.

"Maybe next time, Mrs. Zimmerman," Reid said with a smile.

She let out an exaggerated sigh. "Promises, promises."

He put the mower in the garage, then returned to Katelyn. "Were you just in the neighborhood?" he wondered.

"In the neighborhood…hoping to see you."

Suddenly his day was looking brighter. "Do you want to go inside where we can talk without an audience?"

She hesitated, and he knew she was thinking about Mrs. Clayton and Mrs. Zimmerman and worried what they might think if she was seen going into Reid's apartment.

"It's not even eleven—too early for them to suspect we're going inside for a nooner."

His teasing remark earned a small smile, though she didn't look entirely convinced. Her decision was made easier when Frieda grumbled about preferring to be inside with the air conditioning if there was nothing to see outside and the two old women abandoned their posts.

As Kate followed Reid into his apartment, she could see the perspiration glistening on his skin. She'd never thought she would find a sweaty man appealing, but she couldn't deny that the sight of Reid, his T-shirt stretched over those broad shoulders, a dark V dampening both the front and the back of the fabric, made everything inside her quiver.

"Why do you wear jeans to cut the grass in this heat?" she wondered.

"Because the mower might kick up stones or other debris."

Which made sense but was still disappointing, because his legs could rival his shoulders for Beverly's and Frieda's attention—and even her own.

And then, as if he could hear her thoughts, he lifted the hem of his T-shirt and pulled it over his head, then rubbed the fabric across his chest. Her gaze followed his movements, admiring those incredible shoulders, the sculpted pecs, the rippling abs.

"What are you doing?" she croaked through dry lips.

"I thought you'd probably appreciate it if I took a shower."

"Well, undress in the bathroom," she suggested.

His brows lifted. "I only took off my shirt. And you have seen me naked before."

Yeah, but she couldn't let herself think about "before"— when she'd been naked with him—because she was now dealing with an overload of pregnancy hormones that made her want to do all kinds of wickedly wonderful things to him. And let him do anything he wanted to her in return.

"Of course, it's been a while, hasn't it, Katelyn?" he prompted.

Twenty-two days.

Not that she was counting—not really.

But she was staring—she couldn't seem to help herself.

And the amusement that danced in the depths of those hazel eyes left absolutely no doubt that he was aware of the effect he had on her.

"Do you want to join me in the shower?" he asked. "You're looking a little…flushed."

She swallowed. "I'm fine."

He shrugged, and the casual rise and fall of those amazing shoulders nearly made her whimper.

"Why don't you go relax in the living room then?" he suggested as an alternative.

"I'm fine," she said again, unwilling to go anywhere near the flowered sofa where she'd been naked with him twenty-two days ago.

His quick grin confirmed that he knew what she was thinking. "There are cold drinks in the fridge and ice-cream bars in the freezer. Help yourself to whatever you want."

What she wanted was standing in front of her, but succumbing to that desire—again—would complicate her life exponentially. Instead, she waited to hear the bathroom door close, then went to the freezer to see what kind of ice cream he had.

A few minutes later, Kate heard the water running—a sound that elicited mental images of Reid's naked body. She could picture droplets of water sliding over those perfectly sculpted muscles, caressing his taut skin.

Only when she felt ice cream dripping onto her hand did she shove the images aside and the ice cream into her mouth.

He came out of the bathroom a short while later, wearing a clean T-shirt and a pair of cargo shorts. His hair was still wet from the shower and his jaw was unshaven, and all her girlie parts sighed anew with a combination of pleasure and longing.

He opened the fridge and pulled out a can of cola. "Do you want anything?" he asked her.

Nothing I can have.

But, of course, she just shook her head. "No, thanks."

He popped the tab on the can and lifted it to his mouth to drink. She turned away, wandering toward the living area.

"I thought you were going to get some new furniture."

He shrugged. "It's not a priority right now."

"The last time I was here, you claimed to be allergic to the flowers painted on everything."

He smiled, apparently thinking about the last time she'd been there. "The last time you were here is the reason I've grown quite fond of that sofa—flowers and all."

She felt her cheeks burn.

"Why are you here, Katelyn? Since it's apparently—unfortunately—not for an encore performance."

"I'm here because…I wanted to apologize…for last night."

"Turning down my proposal?"

"Walking away in the middle of our conversation," she clarified. "Apparently pregnancy hormones can cause a woman to become…emotional…and I didn't want to have a breakdown in front of you."

"I can handle a few tears," he assured her. "And I *want* to be there for you—in any way that I can."

"That's the other reason I'm here. I got a call from my doctor's office this morning. Everything's fine," she hastened to assure him. "They were just calling to schedule my first ultrasound."

"Isn't it too soon for an ultrasound? Don't they usually happen between eighteen and twenty weeks?"

"Somebody's been reading up on pregnancy," she mused. "But this is an early scan, to calculate the baby's due date."

"You can't just count the number of weeks from the day the condom broke?"

She shook her head.

"So when are you having this ultrasound?"

"Two o'clock Tuesday at the Battle Mountain Medical Clinic."

"Can I go with you?"

"You can meet me there," she suggested.

"Are you honestly worried that someone might see us together in Battle Mountain?"

"No," she said. "I was actually more concerned that if there was a law enforcement emergency, you might have to take off and leave me stranded."

"I can make it work," he told her.

"Okay, then," she relented. "You can pick me up at one."

Reid was impressed by the modern facility and efficient staff at the Battle Mountain clinic, where they were taken to an exam room only a few minutes after checking in. Katelyn hopped up on the table as instructed, while he was directed to stand on the other side of the table, out of the way but able to see everything that was happening.

A few minutes later, the technician came in and introduced herself to the expectant parents, then briefly outlined the procedure for a transabdominal ultrasound and explained how the measurements she obtained would help accurately pinpoint the baby's estimated date of delivery.

Following her instructions, Katelyn folded back the hem of her top and pushed her yoga pants down to her

hips to expose her abdomen. The technician keyed some
information into the computer, then squirted warm gel
onto the expectant mother's belly. She used what she'd told
them was a transducer—a small plastic device that sent out
and received sound waves (and, in Reid's opinion, looked
a little bit like the upholstery attachment of his vacuum
cleaner)—to spread the gel around.

He reached for Katelyn's hand, a silent gesture of support, and she offered a small smile in return.

Then his attention shifted to the monitor as the tech
clicked the mouse and keyed in the data she was gathering.
But Reid was focused on the grainy black-and-white image
on the screen, searching for something that looked like a
baby. And then he saw it—although it looked more like a
blob than a tiny person. Though on closer inspection, he
could see a head distinct from the body with stubby legs
and little T-Rex arms. But what really struck him when
the technician enlarged the image was that something in
the center of the body blob seemed to be pulsing.

Katelyn was watching, too, her grip on his hand tight-
ening. "What…is that…the baby's heart beating?"

"That's what it is," the technician confirmed.

Then she clicked some more keys, and suddenly the
baby's heartbeat was displayed across the bottom of the
screen, the *woop-woop-woop* surprisingly fast and loud
in the small room.

Reid looked at Katelyn, who was trying to focus on the
screen through eyes blurred with tears. He had a pretty
good idea how she felt, because in the first moment he'd
recognized that big-headed alien-looking blob as their
child, he'd been filled with emotion. And watching and
listening to that little heart beating, he was overwhelmed
by the knowledge that he'd played even a minor part in the
creation of this tiny person.

Later, as he walked out of the medical center beside Katelyn, she reached for his hand. "Thank you for being here with me today."

"Thank you for letting me be here," he said, truly and deeply touched by what he'd experienced—and grateful that she'd included him.

She smiled. "It was pretty amazing, wasn't it? Actually seeing our baby."

He nodded. "For the past few weeks, I've hardly been able to think about anything else. But still, the baby was something vague and distant. Until today. Looking at the image on the screen, hearing the beat of the heart, it suddenly all became real."

"Morning sickness made it real for me," she said lightly. "But I know what you mean. Even though I've experienced changes in my body, they were just abstract symptoms of pregnancy."

He fished his key fob out of his pocket and unlocked the doors of his truck, but he paused before walking Katelyn around to the passenger side. "I know you have all kinds of reasons for believing that marriage isn't necessary or even desirable, but I want our baby to have a real family. I don't want to miss out on the first tooth or first steps because it's not my turn or my day or my weekend. I want both of us to be there for all the milestones."

"I don't want to miss out on anything, either," she admitted. "And if the best way to be sure that doesn't happen is to get married, then let's do it."

"Really?" he asked, equal parts stunned and hopeful. "You mean it?"

She nodded. "I really mean it."

He opened the maps app on his phone. "If we leave now, we can be in Las Vegas in six hours and twenty-two minutes."

But Katelyn shook her head. "We're not getting married today and we're definitely not getting married in Vegas."

"I'm afraid that if we don't do it right now, you might change your mind," he admitted.

"I'm not going to change my mind," she promised.

"Let's make it official, anyway," he said, and pulled a familiar square box out of his pocket. At her questioning look, he shrugged. "What can I say? I'm an eternal optimist."

Then he dropped to his knee again, right there in the parking lot, and said, "Katelyn Gilmore, will you marry me?"

This time, she didn't back away or cut him off. Instead, she held out her hand. "Yes, Reid Davidson, I will marry you."

He rose to his feet and slid the ring on her finger. Then he kissed her, and Kate closed her eyes and let herself be swept away by the romance of the moment.

He kept his arm around her, holding her close for another minute. "Thank you for giving us a chance," he said.

"You might not feel so grateful in another six months, when you haven't had more than three consecutive hours of sleep because our baby's colicky and screaming," she warned.

"Whatever challenges we face, I know we'll get through them together," he assured her.

"The first challenge will be telling my dad."

He opened the passenger door and helped her climb in. "Do you want to do that today?"

"The sooner the better, so we can pick a date and start planning the wedding."

"This weekend works for me," he told her.

"While I appreciate your enthusiasm, if we're going

to get married, we're going to do this right, and not even my family could pull everything together in four days."

"Okay, how much time do you need?"

"More like four weeks," she decided, crossing her fingers that she'd be able to find a wedding dress off-the-rack and the minister would be free and Marcella could squeeze in making a wedding cake and Naomi could do her flowers and—

"So what changed your mind?"

His question was a welcome reprieve from the details spinning through her head—until she realized that he expected an answer.

Because she definitely wasn't ready to tell him the truth—that the reason she'd changed her mind was that she'd fallen in love with him. Not only because she knew he didn't feel the same way but because she suspected it was a truth he wasn't ready to hear.

Since she'd told him about her pregnancy, he'd been focused on doing what was best for their baby. He certainly hadn't said or done anything to hint that he wanted any kind of emotional entanglements. In fact, he'd made it clear he wasn't interested in falling in love.

But she'd seen the look on his face when he saw their baby on the ultrasound monitor—and she recognized the surprise and wonder and love, because they were the same emotions that filled her heart. And if he could fall in love with their unborn child, she had to hope and believe that maybe, someday, he might fall in love with her, too.

Chapter Fourteen

Reid and Katelyn drove straight to the Circle G to share their news with her family. David Gilmore understandably had reservations about the quickness of their engagement—especially when he learned of their plan to marry before the end of the summer.

"Is there any particular reason for the rush?" Katelyn's father asked them.

"I thought you'd want to be a father-in-law before a grandfather," she responded to his question.

"Grandfather?" he echoed, clearly stunned. "You're… pregnant?"

She nodded. "The baby's due in February."

Her father's brow furrowed as he did the math. He looked at Reid, his scowl deepening. "You didn't waste any time making your move, did you?"

"I made the move," Katelyn interjected, attempting to take the heat.

Reid appreciated the effort, but he wasn't going to hide behind his fiancée. "I'd say we moved together," he countered.

She smiled at that. "Maybe we did."

"Well, I guess what matters now is that you're doing the right thing," David said. "Getting married and giving your baby a family."

Reid nodded. "Yes, sir. And it would mean a lot to both of us to have your blessing."

"Well, of course, you've got my blessing," his future father-in-law said. "And my checkbook for the wedding."

"That's a generous offer, sir, but—"

"No buts," David interjected. "I want Katelyn to have the wedding of her dreams—or as close as possible within your time constraints."

She hugged her father. "Thank you."

David smiled at his daughter, his eyes shiny. "Now you better give your grandmother a call—she'll want to know what's going on and help you with the planning."

So Katelyn did, and a short while later her grandparents and siblings showed up to join in the celebration.

It didn't take long after that for the news to make its way through town, and everywhere they went, they were offered congratulations and best wishes. If people were surprised by the August 30 date they'd set for the wedding, they didn't show it to the happy couple.

And they *were* happy.

Reid's only cause for complaint was that he barely saw his bride-to-be in the weeks leading up to the big day. He knew she was busy taking care of all the details that went into a wedding: drafting the guest list and sending out evites, finding a dress, then fittings for the dress, meetings with the baker and the florist, then tracking replies to the invitations and working on a seating plan for the reception—which was being held at the Circle G under the cover of huge tents rented for the occasion.

Reid's responsibilities were limited. He gave his notice to Bev and Norm, since he'd be moving in with Katelyn after the wedding, packed up his meager belongings and went into Elko with Caleb and Liam to be fitted for their tuxes.

Which meant he had a lot of time to focus on his job, which he generally enjoyed. His least favorite part of being sheriff was playing politics. But if he wanted to remain in the position, and of course he did, then he'd need to run for reelection when Jed Traynor's current term expired. And that meant gritting his teeth and making nice with the voters, even when those voters drove him crazy with incessant nuisance calls.

Two days before his wedding, the call was from Ruth Fielding.

"I'll send Deputy Neal to talk to Mr. Petrovsky about his cat digging up your flowers," Reid promised.

"Talking isn't going to grow me new flowers," Ruth protested.

He made a note on the pad on his desk. "Perhaps some form of restitution can be arranged."

"We need a leash law for cats," she said. "I have to put my Harvey on a leash when I take him out. It's not fair that obnoxious feline—"

A movement at the door caught his eye and he looked up, a ready smile on his face for his fiancée, who was meeting him for lunch.

The smile froze on his lips when he saw that it wasn't his soon-to-be wife standing in his doorway, but his ex.

"—gets to run free around the neighborhood and create havoc—"

"You're right, Mrs. Fielding," he interrupted. "And I'll send Deputy Neal over right after lunch."

Then he disconnected the call to focus on his unexpected visitor.

"Trish—what are you doing here?"

She shook her head, a gesture of undisguised exasperation. "Reid, you're getting married in two days—where else would I be?"

"Home in Echo Ridge with your husband and child?" he suggested.

"They came with me," she said. "Because Jonah understands why I needed to be here."

"I'm glad someone does," he said, but he pushed away from the desk and embraced her. "You look good."

"It's the boobs." She smiled proudly as she glanced down at her chest. "Breastfeeding has added a full cup size."

He winced. "Please spare me the details."

"This town needs a decent hotel," Trish said. "We're staying in Battle Mountain because Dusty Boots Motel sounds like a place that rents rooms by the hour and I wasn't sure that you'd have space for us to squeeze in at your place."

His head was spinning. He was grateful that she hadn't made any assumptions about staying with him—which would have been more than a squeeze—but he had to ask, "But why are you here?"

"Did you really think you could send me a text message telling me that you were getting married and not expect some follow-up conversation?"

"I thought you might call," he acknowledged.

"I wanted to read the expression on your face when you explained to me how this happened."

"I met a girl, I asked her to marry me, she said yes."

Trish shook her head. "That's a very concise summary—too concise."

And then he heard a familiar voice in the outer office as Katelyn and Judy exchanged pleasantries.

Reid had no idea how the next few minutes would play out, but he didn't have a good feeling.

"I really wish you'd called before you got on a plane," he muttered.

"If I'd called, you would've told me not to come," Trish acknowledged.

"You're right," he confirmed.

"Which is why I didn't call," she said logically.

"Did it ever occur to you that showing up—unannounced and uninvited—might not go over well with your ex-husband's bride-to-be?"

"No," she admitted. "Why would she care? She's the woman you're head over heels for and I'm already married to someone else."

"I don't know that she will care, but—" he gave up trying to explain as his fiancée walked into his office.

"Sorry, I'm late, I got caught—oh," Katelyn's explanation cut off abruptly when she realized Reid wasn't alone. "I'm sorry. I didn't mean to interrupt."

"You're not interrupting," he assured her.

She looked from him to the other woman in his office and back again.

"Katelyn, this is my ex-wife, Trish."

Whatever she was thinking or feeling, Katelyn kept it hidden behind a neutral expression. But she took a step toward Trish and held out a hand. "It's nice to meet you."

"And you," Trish said, shaking the proffered hand. "I'm really looking forward to getting to know you."

"That's going to have to wait." Katelyn offered a polite if cool smile. "I've got to run to a meeting with a client."

"But we're supposed to have lunch," Reid reminded her.

"I got the call just as I was heading over here—that's why I was late," she said.

And though it was a plausible explanation, he didn't believe it was a complete one.

"We can go after your meeting then," he offered.

Katelyn shook her head. "I really don't know how long I'll be. It's probably better if you two go ahead."

"I could go for lunch," Trish said as Katelyn disappeared out the door. "You pick the place, and I'll pick up the tab."

Reid decided to let her, because he instinctively knew that he'd be paying for this later.

When Kate checked her phone, there were half a dozen missed calls and an equal number of text messages from Reid. She replied to the last one, letting him know that her meeting had gone late but confirming that she was home now.

He immediately responded: I'll bring dinner.

Which dashed any hope of putting him off until the next day.

Ten minutes later, he knocked at the door. Though she'd given him a key because he'd be moving in after the wedding, he wasn't yet in the habit of letting himself in.

She put a smile on her face and opened the door.

Reid walked in carrying a large takeout bag from Diggers', and the scent of spicy buffalo sauce and fried grease teased her nostrils and made her stomach growl.

"I'm guessing you never got around to having lunch today," he said, proof that he'd heard the rumble.

"I guess I didn't," she admitted, only realizing it now herself.

He carried the bag of food to the table.

"Why'd you run out of my office today?"

"I didn't run," she denied, opening the cutlery drawer. "I had a meeting."

He reached in the cupboard beside the sink for plates. "Since when is Emerson a client?"

"Since today," she told him.

Because she was a terrible liar, and because she hated the idea of lying to Reid, she'd made her friend give her a dollar as a retainer so she could legitimately claim solicitor-client privilege and not have to admit that seeing her soon-to-be husband cozied up in his office with his ex-wife had sent her to her best friend's house in tears.

"How'd you know I was with Emerson?"

"Because after I had lunch with Trish—and thanks for setting that up, by the way—"

She bristled at the irritation in his voice as she plucked napkins from the holder on the counter. "No need to thank me," she said. "You're the one who invited your ex-wife to our wedding."

"I didn't invite Trish to our wedding," he told her.

"Then why is she here?"

"Because she has no concept of boundaries."

She set the napkins and cutlery on the table, by the plates he'd already put down.

"I don't know what else to say," he admitted. "I know you're not happy that she's here, but I'm not sure why it bothers you so much."

"Because she's beautiful," Katelyn said glumly.

"Really? That's it?"

She glared at him. "No woman ever wants to meet an ex-girlfriend, lover or wife who looks like she walked off the cover of a magazine."

"It's funny that you'd say that."

"I'm glad you find this amusing."

"Because—" he caught her as she tried to move past him and pulled her into his arms "—Trish told me that no woman, even a happily married new mom, ever wants to discover that she was replaced by a younger and prettier model."

"She really said that?"

"You know I don't understand the workings of a woman's mind well enough to make this stuff up."

"Apparently I'm shallow enough to let that make me feel a little better," she acknowledged. "But I'm still not happy she's here."

"Do you want me to tell her not to come to the wedding?"

"If you do, then she'll know I was the one who didn't want her there, and she came all this way to—"

"Katelyn," he interrupted gently. "This is *our* wedding. What anyone else did or wants doesn't matter if it's not what you want."

She sighed, feeling irrational and unreasonable and generally miserable because nothing about the circumstances of their upcoming marriage were what she would have planned. But of course, none of that was Reid's fault. Or at least none of it aside from getting her pregnant. "What do *you* want?"

"I want you to be happy," he said, and sounded as if he meant it. "And if that means banning my ex-wife and her new husband from our wedding, I'll do it."

Of course, she didn't want her soon-to-be-husband's ex-wife there, but how was she supposed to admit that to him?

"Did you go to her second wedding?" she asked instead.

He nodded. "In the interest of full disclosure, I walked Trish down the aisle when she married Jonah."

"Whose idea was that?"

"Not mine," Reid assured her. "I thought the request

was a little odd but, in the absence of her dad, I didn't see how I could say no."

"What did her new husband think about that?"

"He had no objections. It didn't take him long to realize that me and Trish are more like brother and sister than ex-spouses—and of course he knew the truth about why we got married."

"Because her dad wanted you to take care of her."

He nodded.

"And now you're marrying me because I'm pregnant."

He didn't deny it. If the condom hadn't failed, they might have gone out on a few dates, and maybe those dates might have led to a relationship, but there was no way they'd be planning to marry only two months after he'd moved to Haven.

"Is there a point?" he asked.

"Maybe we shouldn't do this."

"Really? Two days before the wedding, you've suddenly got cold feet?"

"It's not sudden," she said. "You know I've had reservations about this from the beginning."

"But we both agreed that getting married is what's best for the baby."

She nodded. "You're right. But this is the second time you're getting married for the wrong reasons."

"Giving our baby a family isn't a wrong reason."

"You probably didn't think you were marrying Trish for the wrong reason, either, but look how that turned out."

"There are zero similarities between my relationship with Trish and my relationship with you," he told her.

"So why won't you tell me why you split up?"

"I really wish you'd let this go, Katelyn."

"I don't think I can."

He scrubbed his hands over his face. "Trish and I split up because she wanted a baby…and I didn't."

"Oh." Kate now wished she hadn't pushed so hard for an answer to her question.

He lifted his gaze to meet hers again. "Obviously, our situation is completely different."

"How can you say that when you just admitted you didn't want to be a father?" she wondered.

"Because it *is* different," he insisted. "Trish and I were talking about the *possibility* of having a child. The baby you're carrying—*our* baby—is *real*."

"Putting aside that nebulous distinction for now, why didn't you want a child?"

"Because I didn't want to screw up my child the way my parents screwed me up," he confided.

"And now those fears have miraculously disappeared?" she asked dubiously.

"Of course not," he said. "I'm still terrified that I'm going to do something—or a thousand things—wrong. But over the past few weeks, I've started to trust that we can figure it out together."

"I don't want to do this without you," she admitted.

"You don't have to," he promised. "I'm not going into this reluctantly or begrudgingly. I *want* to be your husband and our baby's father. I want to go to sleep beside you at night and wake up next to you in the morning. I want to argue with you about whose turn it is to get up with a screaming baby in the middle of the night. I want to share each and every one of our baby's milestones—the good, the bad and the cranky—with you."

"Even if the cranky part is mine?"

He smiled and touched his lips to hers. "Even if the cranky part is yours."

* * *

One of the difficulties of a midweek ceremony, Kate discovered, was trying to juggle her professional obligations with the final wedding preparations as the days and hours counted down. She was scheduled to meet her attendants—Sky and Emerson—at the spa Tuesday afternoon, but she spent the morning in the office, catching up on some paperwork.

Just before eleven o'clock, Beth poked her head into Kate's office. "Do you have time for a walk-in?"

"Who's the client?"

"A Mrs. Stilton. She didn't say what it was regarding, only that it was important she talk to you today."

"Okay," Kate agreed. She clicked the mouse to save the memorandum she'd been working on, then stood up to greet the client Beth escorted to her office.

The ready smile on her face froze when she recognized Mrs. Stilton as her fiancé's ex-wife.

"Reid didn't tell me your last name."

"I was counting on that to get me in the door," Trish admitted.

"Then you're not here for legal advice?" she guessed.

The other woman shook her head. "No, I wanted to talk to you, woman-to-woman, and this was the only way I could think to make it happen without Reid running interference."

"What did you want to talk about?"

"I wanted to know if you're uncomfortable with the idea of me being at your wedding," Trish said.

"I'm not sure how I feel," Kate admitted.

"I get why it might seem strange to you that we came all the way from Texas for the wedding. And, truthfully, my husband warned me that we might not be welcome."

"I was just…surprised…when I saw you in his office,"

Kate said. "And I did wonder why he didn't tell me you were coming."

"He claims he didn't know," Trish said, confirming what Reid had told Kate. "But he should have known that I'd be on a plane as soon as I heard, because I'm the only family he has.

"And yes, I know that we're not technically family anymore," she continued. "But the connection to my dad created a bond between us. When Reid asked me to marry him, I was under no illusions about his feelings for me. My dad was dying and Reid married me so he wouldn't worry about me being alone.

"Not that I'm not capable of taking care of myself," Trish hastened to clarify. "But my dad was overprotective, and the local sheriff, to boot."

"Believe me, I understand about overprotective parents," Kate said, with a slightly exasperated smile.

"Good, because Reid will probably be even worse when he's a father."

"He told you…about the baby?"

"He didn't need to tell me," the other woman said. "I've known him too long to believe that he'd jump into another marriage without good reason, and in his mind, there's no better reason than to give a baby a family."

Kate nodded, acknowledging the fact.

"And since we're sharing secrets, I'll admit that I had mixed feelings about your pregnancy at first," Trish confided.

"Reid told me why you split up," Kate said.

"So you know I wanted to have a baby and he…had some reservations?"

"He said that he didn't ever want to be a father," Kate clarified.

"He's nothing if not honest," Trish mused. "Sometimes painfully so."

"And yet he's the one who pushed for this wedding."

"Because he's also honorable and loyal—and he wouldn't ever want his child to grow up feeling unwanted."

"Like he did," she realized.

Trish nodded. "When Reid confirmed your pregnancy, I had a moment—it was brief, but still a moment," she confessed, "when I wondered why, if he had to get someone pregnant, it couldn't have been me."

Kate decided that was a reasonable reaction for a woman whose husband hadn't wanted to give her a child.

"But after I had some time to think about it more rationally," the other woman continued, "I realized that Reid and I having a baby together would've been a mistake.

"Maybe we would've stayed together and made our marriage work—he's too loyal and stubborn to believe otherwise—but then I would never have met and fallen in love with Jonah, who really is the love of my life. And Reid would never have met you."

Kate appreciated that Trish didn't pretend to believe her ex-husband had deep feelings for his bride-to-be, but the honesty did sting a little.

"I would like to be there when you exchange your vows," the other woman continued. "But Jonah and I won't show up if our presence is going to make you uncomfortable in any way."

"I'd like you both to be there," Kate decided. "And Henry, too. Reid's made a lot of friends in the short time he's been in Haven, but most of those people knew me— or at least my family—first, so it'll be nice for him to have someone there primarily for him."

"Thank you," Trish said.

"And thank you," Kate said. "For coming here to talk to me, but especially for being here for Reid."

Trish smiled. "I'll see you at the church, soon-to-be Mrs. Reid Davidson."

Chapter Fifteen

Kate and Reid had opted for an evening midweek ceremony to coordinate with the schedule of the minister
who'd married Kate's parents and baptized Kate and each
of her siblings. Unable to choose between her sister and
best friend as her maid or matron of honor, she'd decided
to have both. Because Reid was new in town and didn't
have any close friends to serve as groomsmen, he'd asked
Caleb and Liam to stand up for him.

The bride spent the morning of her wedding day in
court. After that, she had lunch with Skylar and Emerson
before they all headed over to the Circle G together to get
ready for the ceremony.

Her grandmother was waiting at the house when they
arrived—to ensure everyone stayed on schedule, she
claimed.

"You look just like a fairy-tale princess," Emerson said,
when she'd finished tying the corset back of the bride's
dress.

Kate turned to look at her reflection in the mirror, pleased with the overall effect. Her dress was an A-line strapless gown with chapel-length train. The side-drape helped disguise the subtle swell of her belly and the pearl-and-crystal beading on the bodice did make her feel a little bit like a princess.

But before she got too caught up in the fantasy, she reminded herself that Reid wasn't her prince—he was just a guy who wanted to do the right thing. And she knew he'd do everything in his power to make their marriage work—for the sake of their baby. She also hoped that, over time, he'd start to care for her as she cared for him.

She couldn't pinpoint an exact moment when her feelings for him had started to grow and change. There was no denying that the initial attraction had been purely physical, and that attraction was still there. His smile never failed to make her knees weak, the most casual of his touches made her heart pound, and those shoulders...just thinking about those shoulders made her sigh.

But he was also smart and kind and funny. Sure, he could be a little rigid at times and more than a little stubborn, but the more time she'd spent with him, the more she'd suspected that he was a man she could fall in love with. Until the day she'd cut off his marriage proposal, because she'd realized that she'd already fallen.

And in just a few more hours now, she was going to be his wife.

After Emerson's assessment, Grams looked the bride up and down, then shook her head. "Something's missing."

"Flowers," Sky said. "Dad went into town to pick them up."

Grams shook her head again. "Earrings."

Kate instinctively reached a hand to her ear, where she'd fastened the simple diamond studs that had been a gift from her father for her eighteenth birthday. "I'm wearing earrings."

"With your hair up, you should have something a little… more," Grams said, as she took a small fabric pouch out of her pocket. "I know you're wearing Emerson's veil as your something borrowed, but these could be your something old—if you want them."

"Grams, they're gorgeous," Kate said, admiring the delicate diamond-and-pearl drops in her grandmother's hand.

"They were a gift to me from your grandfather on our wedding day, fifty-eight years ago, so they're definitely old," she said. "But they were also your mom's something borrowed when she married your dad."

"Oh." She swallowed hard and blinked back the tears that threatened as she unfastened her diamond studs.

Kate had been thinking of her mom throughout the day, missing her as she always did when she celebrated a milestone event. But as she fastened the pretty pearl-and-diamond drops to her ears, the knowledge that her mother had worn the very same earrings on her wedding day made her feel a little less lonely for her.

"Now you're perfect," Grams declared.

"You're going to knock his socks off," Emerson said approvingly.

"Hopefully a lot more than his socks."

"Grams!" Skylar protested.

Her grandmother just grinned as a knock sounded on the door.

"Flower delivery," her father announced.

"Just on time." Grams took the box from him and distributed the bouquets of hand-tied calla lilies before ushering Skylar and Emerson out of the room so Kate could have a few minutes alone with her father before they headed to the church.

"Oh, Katie." It was all he said, but there was a wealth of emotion in those two words.

"Don't you dare make me cry," she warned her father.

He smiled, though his own eyes were suspiciously bright. "You're so beautiful." Then he touched a finger to one of the dangling earrings. "Your mother wore those the day we got married."

She nodded. "They were her something borrowed from Grams—and now they're my something old."

"Your mom would be so proud of you today. Always," he amended. "But especially today."

"I miss her," she said softly. "Always, but especially today."

"It took me a long time to accept that she was gone, and though the grief has lessened over the years, I will never stop loving her."

Kate pulled a tissue from the box on the dressing table and dabbed at her eyes.

"My greatest wish for you and Reid is to be as happy as we were together."

She kissed his cheek. "Thank you."

"Now, we better be on our way to the church if you don't want to keep your groom waiting. But if you do…" He let the sentence trail off, an unspoken question.

She shook her head. "I'm ready to start the rest of my life with the man I love."

Her response seemed to satisfy her father, who nodded brusquely. "Well then, let's go."

Half an hour before the ceremony was scheduled to begin, Caleb and Liam left the groom to perform their duties ushering guests to their seats.

A short while later, when Reid heard the knock on the door of the anteroom where he was getting ready, he assumed it was one of Katelyn's brothers. But when he said, "Come in," it was Trish who poked her head around the door.

"Have you worn out the carpet yet?" she teased.

"I'm not pacing—I'm trying to pin this flower thing on my jacket," he told her.

"It's a boutonniere," she said. "And the flower is a calla lily."

"Can you help me?"

"Sure," she said, taking the flower from his hand and sizing him up. "You clean up pretty good, Sheriff."

"I'm more comfortable wearing my badge than a suit," he confided.

"The suit looks good on you. Or maybe it's the impending nuptials that look good on you." She positioned the flower on his lapel, slid the pin into the stem—and swore when she pushed too far and stabbed herself.

"You're nervous," he realized.

"A little," she admitted.

"Why are *you* nervous?"

"Because I really want this to work for you, Reid."

He lifted a brow. "And you think I'm going to screw it up?"

"I think you sometimes hold too much back," she told him.

"I think you sometimes share too much," he countered drily.

"I know I do," she acknowledged. "But we're not talking about me—we're talking about you."

"You're nagging me." He handed a corsage box to her when she finished with his boutonniere. "And on my wedding day, too."

"What's this?"

"Katelyn asked me to give it to you."

She looked at the flower inside the box, then at him. "Why?"

He shrugged. "I don't remember exactly what she said—something about traditions and honoring family members who aren't in the wedding party."

"Oh." Trish's eyes filled with tears. "Damn, I really do like that girl."

"I like her, too," he said.

"She's probably too good for you," his ex-wife warned.

"Probably," he agreed easily.

"And yet, I think she could be exactly what you need—if you let her in."

"I'm marrying her, Trish. I'm not sure how much more 'in' there is."

She sighed. "Well, hopefully you'll figure it out."

And with those last cryptic words, she kissed his cheek and walked out of the anteroom.

A short while later, Caleb and Liam returned, then the minister summoned them all to take their positions at the front of the church. The pews were filled with invited guests and other well-wishers from the community, and the pianist was playing something Reid vaguely recognized but couldn't have named.

Emerson came down the aisle first, wearing a strapless lavender dress and carrying a bouquet of long-stemmed flowers that matched the one he was wearing. She winked at him as she took her place on the opposite side of the aisle. Sky followed a few steps behind Emerson, wearing the same style of dress in a slightly darker shade of purple and carrying a similar bouquet. She gave him a quick thumbs-up as she took her place beside Emerson.

The music changed—and Reid's heart started to pound harder and faster against his ribs. Then, finally, the bride was there, at the back of the church, and Reid felt as if all the air had been sucked out of his lungs.

He vaguely registered the presence of her father beside her, but his focus was on Katelyn—absolutely, undeniably the most beautiful bride he'd ever seen.

He didn't know enough about fashion to know the fabric or style of her dress, he only knew that the sparkly bodice hugged her breasts and the skirt trailed behind her as she made her way down the aisle toward him. Her hair was pinned up in one of those fancy knots that always made him want to unpin it, but today there were loose strands that framed and softened her face. In her left hand, she held a bouquet of lilies. Her right was tucked into the crook of her father's arm.

When they reached the altar, David lifted the delicate veil away from her face and leaned in to kiss her cheek, whispering something in her ear that made her lips curve in a tremulous smile. Then the bride's father offered his hand to the groom before stepping back and taking his seat in the front pew.

"We are gathered together today to celebrate the relationship of Katelyn Theresa Gilmore and Reid Thomas Davidson by joining them in marriage…"

Reid held Katelyn's hand and her gaze throughout the ceremony.

The vows he made to her weren't new, but he wanted her to know that they were true. Maybe he didn't love her, but he would honor and cherish her for the rest of their days together.

When they'd both recited the requisite lines and exchanged rings, the minister said, "I now pronounce you husband and wife." Then he nodded to Reid before addressing his next words to Katelyn. "You may kiss your groom."

Reid lifted his brows in response to the not-quite-traditional instruction; Katelyn only smiled as she pulled his mouth down to hers.

"I can't believe you managed to put together this wedding in four weeks," Reid said to his bride as they finished distributing pieces of wedding cake to their guests.

"There are some benefits to being a Gilmore in Haven."

"Such as rewriting the minister's lines?"

"It was a minor amendment, and Pastor Richards likes to go off script sometimes, just to make sure the congregation is paying attention."

"But kissing the bride is the part a groom looks forward to," he said. "So I kind of feel like I was ripped off."

"Do you really need to be told when you can kiss your bride?"

"No," he said, drawing her closer to him. "One of the benefits of putting a ring on your finger is that I get to kiss you whenever I want."

"You think so, do you?"

"Yes, I do," he confirmed.

And he kissed her then to prove it.

"I think I'm going to like being married to you," Katelyn said when he finally ended the kiss.

"I hope so, because you're going to be stuck with me for a very long time." He gestured to the dance floor where her grandparents were dancing, cheek to cheek. "That's going to be us in fifty years."

"They've been married fifty-eight years," she told him.

"They're an inspiration, that's for sure."

"My parents were the same," Katelyn said. "After my mom died, there were days I wasn't sure my dad would survive the grief of losing her."

"It couldn't have been easy on any of you."

"It wasn't," she confirmed. "But they were so…connected.

Like two halves of a whole, each one incomplete without the other. They met at The Silver State Stampede and immediately fell in love, and there was never any question in either of their minds or hearts that it was forever."

He knew that she'd wanted the same thing—love at first sight and happily-ever-after. And though he was sorry she'd had to compromise her ideals, he intended to do everything in his power to ensure she wouldn't ever regret it.

"Even if it wasn't love at first sight between us, there was definite lust at first sight," he said, attempting to lighten the mood.

She tipped her head back, a smile tugging at the corners of her mouth. "At first sight?"

"Oh, yeah," he confirmed. "The minute you walked into that conference room, a hint of black silk peeking above the button of that blue jacket, the matching skirt displaying mouthwatering long legs that went all the way down to sexy black shoes with heels that put your mouth almost level with mine."

"That's some detailed recollection," she noted.

"You caught my attention," he assured her. "And then you invited me back to your room."

"There were a couple of steps in between," she noted. "But the minute I saw you, I wanted you, too. In fact, the prospect of sharing a bed with you weighed heavily in the yes column when I was considering your proposal."

He smiled. "And you said 'click' wasn't a factor."

"I've reconsidered my position on the matter. In fact, I'm hopeful that later we'll be sharing a naked and horizontal position."

He lifted a brow. "You've got ambitious plans for tonight."

"It *is* our wedding night," she reminded him. "And I

don't think anyone at our respective offices would be surprised if we were a little late for work tomorrow."

"About that," Reid said, withdrawing an envelope from his jacket pocket.

"What's this?"

"Open it and see," he suggested.

She lifted the flap to peek inside. "A travel itinerary?"

"I know we said we shouldn't take any time away right now," her new husband acknowledged, "but Connor promised that he could handle anything that came up in the Sheriff's Office through the weekend and Beth managed to clear your schedule for a few days so that we can have a honeymoon, albeit an abbreviated one."

She pulled the pages out to scan them more closely. "The flight is at 5:50 in the morning?"

"Yeah, so we won't be sleeping in tomorrow. In fact, we're probably going to want to skip out of the party early tonight."

"Or now," she said, sounding excited and just a little bit panicked. "We need to go home and pack."

"I've already packed my bag, your sister packed one for you and our boarding passes are printed."

"You've thought of everything."

"I know this isn't exactly the wedding day of your dreams," he told her. "But I wanted to do it right, as much as possible under the circumstances, and not having a honeymoon just didn't seem right."

"Why San Francisco?"

"It's relatively simple to get there from here, it's close enough that we won't lose a lot of time traveling, and it's one of your favorite cities."

"How did you know that?"

"I asked Emerson for some help with the planning," he admitted. "And bribed her not to breathe a word about it to you—and since your reaction assures me that she didn't, I'm going to be carting a ton of Ghirardelli chocolate back from San Francisco."

"Make that two tons," she said.

"You can cart your own chocolate," he teased.

"It's not for me," she said. "It's for the baby."

"You're going to milk that for the next five-and-a-half months, aren't you?"

"As much as possible," she promised.

He smiled as he dipped his head and touched his lips to hers. "Let's go say goodbye to our guests and get this honeymoon started."

As eager as Kate had been to get back to her apartment— *their* apartment—and get naked with her new husband, now that they were alone together, she suddenly felt shy.

Reid shrugged out of his jacket and tossed it over the reading chair in the corner of her—*their*—bedroom.

"Are you tired?" he asked, somehow sensing her hesitation.

"Tired but not sleepy," she said. It had been a long day, and her limbs were weary but her blood was humming with nerves and anticipation.

"The sugar from that cake should keep you revved for a while—" he grinned as he unfastened his tie "—I hope."

She watched as his nimble fingers made quick work of the buttons that ran down the front of his shirt. Her mouth went dry when the fabric parted, revealing a strip of beautiful, bronzed skin.

"Do you need a hand with your dress?" he asked.

"Probably," she admitted. "Emerson tied up the corset, so I'm not sure how to get out of it."

"I think getting my wife out of her clothes is going to be one of my favorite husbandly duties," he said.

"You might not think so in a few months." She turned her back to him, so he could see how the dress was done up.

"I will always think so," he promised, starting to work on the corset.

When the lace had been loosened and the bodice began to drop, she caught and held it in place.

He didn't say anything about her impeding his efforts but only dropped his head to press a kiss to her bare shoulder. The brush of his lips on her skin raised goosebumps on her flesh.

Then he kissed her again, midway between her shoulder and her neck. And again, at the base of her throat.

She shivered.

"Your skin is so soft…so sweet."

Her eyes closed as his mouth moved up her throat, skimmed over her jaw.

"I want to taste you—" he teased her lips "—all over."

Heat pulsed in her veins, melting her resistance.

She let go of the bodice and wriggled out of the dress.

He stroked his hands down her sides, his thumbs gently caressing the slight swell between her hipbones.

"There's our little bean," he said, his tone soft, almost reverent.

"Actually, our baby is the size of a lemon now."

He shook his head. "Little bean sounds better than little lemon."

"Is our baby still going to be 'little bean' when he or she is the size of a honeydew melon?"

He eased her back onto the bed. "Are you growing a baby in there or making a fruit salad?"

"A baby," she assured him.

"*Our* baby," he clarified, then pressed his lips to the curve of her belly.

"Some men are…turned off by the changes in a woman's body during pregnancy," she said cautiously.

"Some men are idiots."

His blunt response made her smile, but still, she wasn't convinced he knew what he was in for.

"This is still the early stages," she warned. "When our baby is the size—"

He touched his fingers to her lips. "I know your body is going to change as our baby grows inside you, but getting naked with you is always going to be a huge turn-on for me."

"Really?" she said dubiously.

"Really," he confirmed. "You are beautiful and amazing and the sexiest woman I've ever known, and it's going to give me infinite pleasure to prove it to you throughout the next five-and-a-half months and beyond. Starting—" his hands moved to her breasts, already a little fuller and a lot more sensitive, his thumbs tracing around the areola "—now."

That night, all through the night, Kate learned that her husband was a man of his word.

Chapter Sixteen

Kate had always loved California—Sacramento and San Diego and every stop in between—but San Francisco was one of her all-time favorite cities. From the Golden Gate Bridge and the sparkling waters of the Bay to Lombard Street and the cable cars, Chinatown and Fisherman's Wharf, there was so much to see and do that she never got bored. And because Reid had never been to the city, she was able to see it again for the first time through his eyes.

Of course, the sheriff wanted to go to Alcatraz, and his wife did not. She told him, without regret, that there wouldn't be any last-minute tickets available during tourist season, because it was usually true. But the hotel concierge worked some magic and Reid presented her with two tickets for the ferry to the infamous island prison—cleverly hidden in a basket of Ghirardelli chocolate. It was a blatant bribe, but one she couldn't refuse, so they went to the island, toured the prison and the grounds, the former being much creepier and the latter much prettier than she'd anticipated.

Another day, they walked to Pier 39 to see the sea lions sunning on the docks and enjoy the talents of street performers. Later, they browsed the shops at Fisherman's Wharf, ate fresh shrimp out of plastic cups from a local food truck and sourdough rolls from the Boudin Bakery. They rented bicycles and cycled across the bridge, walked hand in hand through Golden Gate Park and took a cable car to Union Square to browse the upscale shops.

And when they finally went back to their hotel room, they made love, every night.

The morning sickness that had plagued her daily for several weeks had passed long ago, though it continued to make an occasional appearance—including their last morning in San Francisco.

Reid set their packed cases beside the door and did a quick check around the room to ensure they hadn't forgotten anything.

"Looks like we're good to go," he said.

Kate nodded hesitantly as her stomach decided it was unhappy with the brioche French toast and fresh fruit cup that had tasted so good only half an hour earlier.

"Katelyn?" he prompted.

"I'm sorry, but—" That was all she managed before she raced to the bathroom and slammed the door.

Reid knew she'd suffered from morning sickness earlier in her pregnancy, but she'd told him—with her fingers crossed—that the nausea had finally subsided. Listening to her retch through the door, he thought that her crossed fingers might have been a little premature.

"Katelyn?" He jiggled the handle of the door, frowning when it refused to turn. She'd been in a hurry to reach the toilet but she'd still managed to lock him out.

"Just give me a minute."

He heard the toilet flush, then the water turn on.

He rummaged through the suitcase for her toiletry bag, pulled out her toothbrush and toothpaste and had them waiting when she unlocked and opened the door again.

"Thanks," she said, not looking at him as she retreated with the items into the bathroom again.

They'd planned to take the BART to the airport, but Reid called the front desk and asked for a cab instead, which bought them a few extra minutes and gave his wife a little more privacy to feel miserable. He also took the plastic liner for the ice bucket and tucked it into his pocket, just in case.

When she came out of the bathroom, she looked tired and pale—not at all like a woman who'd enjoyed her brief holiday. She tucked her toothbrush and paste away again and zipped up the suitcase.

"Sorry for the delay," she said.

"Why are you apologizing?"

"Because I've put us behind schedule and if we miss the train, we'll be late checking in for our flight and—"

"There's a cab waiting for us downstairs," he said.

"To take us to the train station?"

"To take us to the airport."

"That's going to cost a fortune."

"Only a small one," he said. "And worth it, because we won't feel rushed and you'll be able to close your eyes and relax for a little while."

"You're taking care of me, aren't you?"

"I'm trying to," he admitted. "But you don't make it easy."

She didn't respond to that.

"One of the reasons we got married was so that we

could raise our child together. Until the baby's born, we both need to take care of you."

"I'll never object to you taking care of our vomiting child," she promised. "But I don't want anyone watching me throw up. It's humiliating enough to know that you could hear me yakking my breakfast into the toilet."

"In sickness and in health," he reminded her.

"I'm not sick, I'm pregnant, and I really thought the morning sickness had passed. I was throwing up almost every day for a few weeks, then it was just once every two or three days, and for the past couple of weeks, it's only been once a week. The last time was last Sunday, so I probably should have been prepared for this today."

"Then it wasn't because we overdid it these past few days?"

She shook her head. "No. I'm sure the nausea isn't linked to anything we did or ate, and I sincerely hope the last half hour isn't what you remember when you think about our honeymoon in San Francisco."

"It won't be," he promised. "I loved being here with you and seeing the sights, but my favorite memories took place in this room—most of them in that king-size bed."

"Maybe we should get a bigger bed—if you think one would fit in the apartment," she suggested.

"I don't mind a queen," he said. "It makes us snuggle closer."

"You'll be closer than you want when my huge belly's taking up all the space between us. I already feel like this baby's getting bigger and bigger every day."

He laid his hands on the slight curve of her belly. "Coincidentally, you get more and more beautiful every day."

"We'll see if you still think so in five months."

"I'll still think so in five months," he promised. "And in five years and in fifty years."

And although he said the words to reassure her, he realized that he meant them.

Yeah, he'd proposed to Katelyn because she was pregnant, and he'd campaigned for her to say yes because he wanted to be more than a part-time father to their child. But sometime over the past few weeks, his motivation had stopped being all about the baby. Over the past few weeks, he'd realized that his life was fuller, richer and happier with Katelyn—so much so that he didn't want to imagine a future without her in it.

Kate was surprised by how easy it was to settle into the routines of married life once they got back to Haven.

Although the legal union between a criminal defense attorney and the local sheriff meant that there were some inherent conflicts between them, they adopted a strict rule about leaving work at the office to ensure that nothing interfered with either of them doing their respective jobs. She was fired by one long-time client who didn't believe she could continue to represent him fairly, but for the most part, her practice continued to grow—and so did the baby.

Aiden Hampton had finished his community service before returning to school for the fall term of his senior year, but he and his father continued to attend the grief counseling sessions that had been recommended by the Diversion Program coordinator. Near the end of September, the teen appeared in court for the final dismissal of the charges against him, after which he thanked the judge, then his attorney and even the sheriff who had locked him up—if only for a few hours.

"Do you have to rush back to the office?" Reid asked Kate when court had been dismissed.

She shook her head. "There's nothing that can't wait until tomorrow."

"Good, then you can take a ride with me."

She hitched her briefcase on her shoulder and walked beside him out of the courthouse. He guided her to his personal truck rather than the official vehicle of the Sheriff's Office and opened the passenger door for her. "Where are we going?"

"It's a surprise," he told her.

"What's a surprise?" she pressed.

He just shook his head. "No one warned me about your impatience before I married you."

"You think I'm impatient? Just wait until there's a child strapped into a car seat in the back asking, 'Are we there yet?' every two minutes," she said.

"I can wait," he said, flicking on his indicator before turning into a distinctly residential area. "Because I'm not impatient."

"Are we there yet?" she asked:

He turned again, onto a dead-end street, then pulled up alongside the curb in front of a two-story brick house with a For Sale sign in the front yard.

"Yes," he said. "We're there."

Kate felt a flutter of excitement in her belly as she looked at the house. She was familiar with the neighborhood, of course. There were newer and fancier homes being built on the south side of town, but this area was established, with bigger lots, plenty of mature trees and within walking distance of both the elementary and secondary schools.

"I know the apartment is really convenient to your office and the courthouse," he said to her. "But it's kind of small—plus it was yours before it was ours, so I thought maybe we could choose another place together. Somewhere with room to grow."

"Hey, I haven't put on that much weight," she protested.

He chuckled softly. "I meant to grow our family. Don't you think little bean should have a brother or sister someday?"

She felt the telltale sting of tears behind her eyes. "You want to have another baby with me?"

"Yeah," he said. "I didn't have any siblings growing up, but watching you with yours, I've learned to appreciate the bond you share, and I want that for our kids."

"Brothers and sisters are great," she agreed. "When they're not a total pain in the a—"

He touched a finger to her lips. "Didn't we agree not to use bad language around the baby?"

"Do you really think our baby is hearing anything yet?"

"The books say that babies start to hear sound at eighteen weeks."

"Even if he—or she—can hear what I'm saying, I doubt he—or she—is comprehending," she said drily.

"I'd rather not take any chances that his—or her—first word might be an inappropriate one."

She linked her arms behind his head. "You're going to be a great dad."

"I'm going to do my best," he promised.

"So…how many kids were you thinking you'd like to have?"

"At least two," he said.

"You might change your mind after the first one's born," she warned. "When you've gone a month with no more than two consecutive hours of sleep and you've changed so many diapers you've lost count."

"Trish called today, didn't she?"

Kate nodded.

"You really need to start screening your calls," he advised.

"I like talking to her," she said. "Usually."

He turned her back toward the house. "What do you think? Do you want to look inside?"

"Don't we have to wait for the real estate agent?"

He shook his head. "I've got the code for the lockbox."

"I guess, since you're the sheriff, she figured you were trustworthy?"

"Good guess," he said, leading her to the front door.

"It needs some work," he warned as he turned the key in the lock. "But mostly cosmetic—fresh paint, maybe new carpet or hardwood, updated appliances—and we could take care of that before we moved in."

As he showed her around the empty house—the owner having already moved to Arizona for a job promotion—she had to agree with his assessment. The decor was a little outdated, but she liked the layout—and she loved the spaciousness of the kitchen and the fireplace in the living room and the master bedroom suite.

"What do you think?" he asked, ending the tour at the backyard, slightly overgrown with grass and weeds.

"It might need more work than you realize, once you scrape off wallpaper and pull up carpets," she warned. "Are you sure you're ready to tackle all of that?"

"I want to tackle all of that," he told her. "I want our kids to have a house with a backyard, the lawn scattered with toys, maybe a swing set or one of those climbing things.

"And a dog," he added impulsively. "We should definitely get a dog."

"Let's see how we manage with a baby first," she suggested.

"But what about the house?" he prompted.

And his expression was so hopeful and his enthusiasm so infectious, she threw caution to the wind. "Let's do it."

Ten days later, they signed the final papers and got the keys. That night, they picked up pizza from Jo's and took it to 418 Sagebrush Lane, where they sat on the floor of the living room and ate their first meal in their new home. But they agreed it would be easier to do the work they wanted done before they moved in, and they'd set an ambitious target date of the end of October.

"Speaking of dates," Kate said, as she wiped pizza sauce off her fingers with a napkin. "It's our one-month anniversary tomorrow."

"Is that something we're supposed to celebrate?"

"Not formally," she said. "But I thought I might actually cook something for dinner—and you could pick up caramel fudge brownie cheesecake from Sweet Caroline's for dessert—and we could have a private celebration."

"I like the sound of that," he agreed.

So Kate talked to Emerson and got a recipe that her friend promised was relatively foolproof. After work, she stopped by The Trading Post to get everything she needed to prepare the meal and then meticulously followed her friend's step-by-step instructions.

Half an hour later, when everything was finally ready, she got a text message from Reid.

Sorry. Got a call. Won't make dinner.

She immediately replied:

Ok. Be safe.

Because as disappointed as she was that their plans for the evening had been ruined—or at least delayed—she understood that being married to the local sheriff inevitably meant there would be times when he didn't make it home for dinner. It was even possible that, his best intentions notwithstanding, he wouldn't be with her when she gave birth.

As if unsettled by that possibility, their baby kicked an angry protest. Well, Kate guessed it was a kick, but all she really felt was a flutter. She was exactly nineteen weeks into her pregnancy now, and Emerson had assured her that what she'd originally described as a feeling of little air bubbles popping inside her belly were actually her baby's first movements.

She couldn't wait until the baby was bigger and those movements were stronger, so Reid could feel them, too. But for now, she put a hand on the curve of her belly, instinctively soothing. "It's okay, little bean. We'll make sure you don't make your grand entrance into the world until Daddy's with us."

Then she went to the kitchen to turn off the stove. And though she wanted to wait to eat with Reid, however late that might be, she scooped some rice into a bowl and added a spoonful of the chicken cacciatore because the baby was hungry now—and desperately craving the cheesecake Reid was supposed to bring home for dessert.

She was putting her empty bowl and fork into the dishwasher when her phone buzzed again.

Anticipating an update from Reid, she immediately snatched it up, only to be disappointed when she saw the message from her answering service.

*Urgent. Client wants to meet asap. 775-555-6728

And Kate figured if Reid was working, she might as well be, too.

She was asleep on the sofa, the baseball game on the television now into extra innings, when Reid got home.

The rich scents of tomato and basil lingered in the air—the remnants of dinner she'd cooked for their one-month anniversary.

His wife.

His brilliant and beautiful, sweet and sexy, amazing and pregnant wife.

Damn, he'd lucked out when he'd signed up for that conference in Boulder City. At the time, he'd considered himself lucky just to get the invitation back to her room. He certainly hadn't been thinking that there might be a wedding and a baby in his future. Truthfully, he probably would have run far and fast if anyone had told him that's where he'd end up, so he was grateful he hadn't known, because now he had everything he never knew he wanted.

He picked up the remote and turned off the TV. Katelyn didn't stir. He lifted her into his arms; she sighed and turned her face into his shoulder. She was almost halfway through her pregnancy now and grumbling about the eight pounds she'd put on. Not that the slight swell of her belly was obvious, but apparently her wardrobe options were shrinking as her waistline expanded.

She was still the sexiest woman he'd ever known. And the changes her body was going through as a result of her pregnancy only made her more appealing.

He loved making love with her. And afterward, he loved to cuddle with his hand on her belly. He loved taking her first cup of coffee—decaf—to her in the morning and exchanging brief text messages with her through the hours they were apart. And he especially loved going home at the end of the day to find her waiting for him.

But did he love her?

He wasn't one to get hung up on words. In his opinion, there was far too much emphasis placed on that one particular phrase and too many people who threw it around frequently and easily.

Truthfully, he didn't know if he loved her, but he would do everything he could to make her happy—though she would claim that she was responsible for her own happiness; to take care of her—though she would insist she didn't need anyone to take care of her; and to protect her—though she would argue that she could protect herself.

Yeah, she could argue the opposite side of any issue, and that was just one more thing he loved about her.

He pulled back the covers and laid her gently on top of the mattress, then quickly stripped out of his clothes and slid into bed beside her.

And fell asleep with her in his arms.

Chapter Seventeen

Katelyn was still sleeping when Reid reluctantly slid out of bed in the morning.

He would have liked to stay with her, but he'd agreed to meet Connor at the Sheriff's Office at eight so they could head to the hospital in Battle Mountain. The young store clerk shot during the robbery at The Trading Post had been in critical condition when he was rushed into surgery the night before. Reid had been in the OR waiting room with the parents when the doctor informed them that the surgery had gone well. An early morning call to the hospital revealed that the victim's condition had been downgraded to "serious but stable" and the sheriff was eager to get his statement.

But first, he brewed Katelyn's decaf coffee, as he did every morning, and carried the mug to the bedroom along with a plate bearing a thick slice of Sweet Caroline's caramel fudge brownie cheesecake.

"Good morning, sleepyhead."

She blinked against the harsh glare of the light when he hit the switch with his elbow, but she pushed herself up in bed and brushed back the hair that was falling into her face.

Her eyes lit up when they zeroed in on his gifts. "You remembered the cheesecake."

He chuckled as he set the mug on the bedside table and relinquished the plate to her eager hands. "Of course, I remembered the cheesecake." Then he leaned over to brush her lips with his. "Happy belated one-month anniversary."

"I'm sorry I didn't stay awake until you got home last night." She picked up the fork and dug into the dessert.

"It's okay," he said. "I'm sorry I was late."

Of course, it wasn't the first time and they both knew it wouldn't be the last.

"You missed really hot anniversary sex," she said around a mouthful of cake.

"I'm even sorrier about that."

"Well, we could have really hot morning-after-the-one-month-anniversary sex…after I finish my cheesecake," she told him.

"Words cannot express how tempted I am," he assured her. "But I'm heading back out with Deputy Neal this morning to do some follow-up to our investigation." He kissed her again. "Rain check?"

"Absolutely," she promised.

Kate didn't complain about Reid having to work, even on a Sunday, because she had plenty to occupy her own time—not the least of which was putting together a defense for her newest client. And though it was just as easy to work on her laptop in the apartment, she generally preferred to work at work.

So after she'd finished her coffee and her cheesecake—
and how great was it to be married to a man who indulged
her pregnancy cravings?—she showered and dressed and
headed to her office.

She only felt a little guilty about representing a suspect in the armed robbery that Reid was investigating.
They'd both known before they got married that their ca-
reers would occasionally put them on opposite sides of the
courtroom, and this was just another one of those times.

She unlocked the office door, punched in the security
code to disarm the alarm system, then locked the door
again behind her and headed into her office.

Beth always emptied the wastebaskets and put the garbage out before she left the office on Friday afternoons,
so when Kate hit the light switch and realized there was
something in the basket beside her desk, she was immediately uneasy. Moving closer, she saw what looked like
a brown paper lunch bag—certainly nothing that would
explain her growing trepidation. But the weight of the basket warned the bag wasn't empty, and she used the tip of
a pen to open it so she could peek inside.

Then she put the wastebasket down again, picked up
the phone and dialed the sheriff's number.

Reid and Connor were leaving Battle Mountain when
Katelyn called, so they stopped at her office before heading to their own. She'd hinted about something that might
be relevant to their investigation, and though Reid couldn't
imagine what it might be, he knew she wouldn't have interrupted him if it wasn't important.

"I didn't touch it."

They were the first words she spoke when they walked
into her office.

"Didn't touch what?" he asked cautiously.

"The gun."

Even without any context, the words gave his heart an unexpected jolt.

"What gun?"

It was Connor who asked the question, as Reid's heart was somewhere in the vicinity of his throat, rendering speech difficult.

She pointed to the trash receptacle beside her desk.

Reid shoved his heart back into his chest, looked into the basket and swore. "How did this get here?"

"I don't know." But her face was pale and there was a slight tremor in her voice. "Beth always takes out the garbage on Fridays, and I didn't have appointments yesterday, but I did, um, meet with a client here last night."

"Who?" Reid demanded.

"You know I can't—"

"Screw solicitor-client privilege," he practically snarled at her. "I want to know who was in *my wife's* office with a weapon."

If he'd been thinking clearly, he would've realized that was the absolute wrong thing to say to her. But he wasn't thinking clearly—he couldn't think past the fact that whoever had callously pulled the trigger to put a bullet in the twenty-three-year-old clerk at The Trading Post had then carried the weapon into Katelyn's office.

Didn't she know that desperate people did desperate things? That the client she was determined to protect could have used the gun on her? Didn't she realize Reid could have left one crime scene and come home to find his wife, not sleeping on the sofa with a baseball game on TV, but bleeding out on the floor in her office?

Just the thought made his whole body break out into a sweat.

But Katelyn only straightened her spine and narrowed

her gaze—a warrior ready for battle. "You do your job, *Sheriff*, and I'll do mine."

He knew her mention of his position was intended to draw a line between them, but it also served to remind him that he was there in his professional capacity—and with his deputy as a witness to their altercation, too.

He drew in a deep breath, battling against the fear and impotence that held him captive, and managed a brisk nod. "I assume you have no objection to us taking this—" he picked up the wastebasket again "—into evidence?"

"Of course not," she said, her tone cool and stiff.

"Why don't I head over to the office to get it logged in and sent to ballistics?" Connor suggested.

"You can both go," Katelyn said, but her gaze never shifted away from Reid's. "I have nothing else to say right now."

"Well, I do." Reid shoved the basket at his deputy.

Connor took his cue—and the evidence—and hurried out the door with only a sympathetic glance in his boss's direction.

"I'm sorry," Reid said, after he heard the exterior door open and close again.

Katelyn sighed and lowered herself into the chair behind her desk. "I know."

"That's it? You're not going to apologize?"

"What am I supposed to apologize for?"

It was a reasonable question, but he still wasn't close to feeling reasonable. "Maybe representing scumbag clients," he suggested. "And, by the way, you are *never* again to meet with any of them here alone at night."

"That's not your call to make," she said, her tone icy.

"If you won't think about your own safety, you should at least think about the baby you're carrying. *Our* baby."

"I would *never* do anything to put our baby at risk."

"Oh, well then, why would I worry?" he said, his voice dripping with sarcasm.

She folded her hands on top of the desk, focusing all her attention on the task of lacing her fingers together. When she spoke again, her voice was carefully neutral. "I think you should probably head back to the Sheriff's Office now."

He decided she was right. They were just going around in circles, he was frustrated by her refusal to acknowledge the recklessness of her behavior, and if he didn't walk away, one of them would say something they'd regret.

Kate blew out a weary breath when Reid finally walked out of her office. She stayed where she was after he'd gone, still shaking—with both fear and fury—and not certain her watery legs would be able to support her if she tried to move.

Thankfully, she'd managed to pull herself together by the time she heard a familiar voice say, "Knock knock," from the outer office.

"I'm back here," she said, hastily wiping at her tears before Emerson came around the corner.

"Hey." Her friend gave her a quick hug. "I had some errands to run in town and saw Reid leaving, so I thought I'd stop by and see how your dinner turned out last night."

"It was a complete bust," Kate admitted.

"He didn't like the chicken?"

"He didn't make it home for dinner."

Emerson frowned. "Why…" And then she put the pieces together. "The shooting at The Trading Post?"

Kate nodded.

"It must be hard, not just having plans ruined but knowing your husband's life could be in danger just because he's doing his job," Emerson said sympathetically.

"Of course I worry about him," she admitted. "But I trust that he'll take all necessary precautions to stay safe and come home at the end of the night. Unfortunately, he doesn't seem to have the same faith in me."

"What do you mean?"

So Kate summarized for her friend the argument they'd had after Reid learned about her meeting with the new client—without revealing any details, of course.

"I know you think he overreacted," Emerson said. "But even I was freaked out listening to the story, and you're not my wife or the mother of my unborn child."

"I'm not unsympathetic to his concerns—I just want him to trust me to do my job the same way I trust him to do his," she said.

"Every marriage has an adjustment period as two people who are used to living their own lives suddenly have to learn to communicate and compromise."

Kate shook her head. "This isn't an adjustment problem."

"What do you think the problem is?"

"He doesn't trust me."

"In all fairness, he doesn't really know you," Emerson said gently. "You've been married for a month, and you dated for only a short time before the wedding."

All of which was true, of course. She sighed. "Maybe I shouldn't have married him."

"Is that really how you feel?" her friend asked.

She considered the question for a moment. Though she and Reid had only been married a few weeks, she already couldn't imagine her life without him in it—she didn't want to imagine her life without him in it. Because despite an overprotective streak that rivaled her father's and a frustrating insistence on doing things for her that she was perfectly capable of doing herself, Reid was the man she loved.

"No," she finally said. "I don't regret marrying him."

"Then you're going to have to be patient—and give yourselves both some time to figure things out."

But it was hard to communicate with a man who was hardly ever around. And after the argument in her office, Reid kept himself busy.

At first Kate thought it was just the ongoing investigation that was monopolizing his time, but when that was complete, he spent every free minute at the new house: stripping wallpaper, tearing out carpets, painting ceilings and baseboards and, after Kate had picked the colors she wanted, walls.

He worked hard—every day. Sometimes he was at the house so late, he would crash on the sofa in the living room when he finally got back to the apartment so as not to disturb Kate's rest. At least that was the excuse he gave, but with every day that passed, she felt the distance between them growing.

She'd stayed away from the renovations, because he was worried the dust from sanding and the smell of paint wouldn't be good for the baby. She decided the distance between them wasn't good for the baby—or their marriage—either.

Ten days after their big argument, and three days before they were scheduled to fly to Texas for Henry's christening, she picked up takeout from Diggers' and took it to the new house.

He looked so sexy in paint-splattered jeans with an old Echo Ridge Sheriff's Office T-shirt stretched across those broad shoulders and a slight hint of stubble darkening his strong jaw—and she missed him like crazy.

"I thought you might want to take a break and have something to eat."

He set the roller in the pan and covered it with the

corner of a plastic drop sheet. "I am hungry," he said. "Thanks."

"Maybe we could sit outside?" she suggested. There wasn't any furniture in the house, but there was a patio set that the former owners had left.

"Sure," he agreed.

"You've been busy out here, too," she noted, as they stepped through the patio doors onto the back deck.

"Norm let me borrow his mower," he said.

"It looks good."

"Better, anyway," he agreed.

She opened the bag of food, handed him a foil-wrapped bacon cheeseburger, a paper sleeve of french fries and a can of cola.

"You're not eating?"

"I had something earlier," she said. Which was true—she just didn't specify that 'earlier' was actually lunch.

"Little bean still craving cheesecake these days?"

She shook her head. "Pineapple mango smoothies."

"A surprisingly healthy choice," he noted.

"Well, it's only been three days," she admitted.

For the next few minutes, he focused on eating, though he nudged the fries toward Kate, silently offering to share.

She selected one and nibbled on the end.

When he'd finished his burger, she ventured to ask, "Are we still going to Echo Ridge on the weekend?"

He picked up the can of soda, sipped. "If you want to."

"Of course I want to."

"Okay then," he said agreeably.

"Do *you* want to?"

"Sure."

He offered her some more fries; she shook her head.

"Are you going to initiate any kind of conversation or just answer my questions as succinctly as possible?"

He popped a couple of fries into his mouth, chewed.

"I heard you talking to Emerson," he finally said. "The day you found the gun, I came back with an evidence receipt, and the two of you were in your office."

"Okay," she said cautiously, trying to remember any part of the conversation that could've caused his withdrawal.

"You said you wished you hadn't married me."

Kate immediately shook her head. "No, I didn't. I don't remember exactly what I said," she admitted. "But I know I wouldn't have said that because it's not true."

"Well, it was something along those lines," he insisted. "And it got me wondering...if you wanted out."

She swallowed, her throat tight. "I don't want out." She folded a paper napkin in half, then again, her heart heavy as she contemplated asking the question she wasn't sure she wanted him to answer. "Do you?"

"No." He answered without hesitation, which loosened the vise around her chest a little. "But I don't want you to be unhappy."

"I'm not unhappy being married to you," she said. Then, remembering what her friend had said about honest communication, she elaborated on her response. "I'm also not happy that my husband of six weeks has apparently moved out of our bedroom."

"I didn't move out of our bedroom," he denied. "But I thought we could both use some space."

"You mean *you* needed some space."

"Maybe I did," he acknowledged.

"Have you almost had enough space?" she asked hesitantly. "Because I'd kind of like my husband back."

"Yeah—" he reached across the table and covered her hand with his "—I've had more than enough space."

The vise loosened a little more. "Since I'm pouring out my heart here, there's something else you should know."

"What's that?" he asked, a little warily.

"I didn't just agree to marry you so our baby would have two parents, but because I wanted a partner to share my life, for the rest of my life. And…because I fell in love with you."

He opened his mouth, then closed it again without saying a word, crushing any tentative hope that he might express similar feelings. And then he withdrew his hand, ostensibly to pick up his soda, but she knew the drink was just a diversion.

She pushed her chair away from the table. "Anyway," she said, pleased that her level tone gave no indication that her heart was breaking. "I just wanted you to know."

Reid let her go.

He sat at the table, the bag of garbage balled up in his fist, and watched her walk away because he was an idiot and a coward.

He should have said something. When a woman told a man she loved him, she expected some kind of response. But he'd said nothing, because he didn't know what to say or what to feel. And yes, because he was afraid—afraid to believe her feelings were real, even more afraid to acknowledge his own.

All the books and articles on pregnancy talked about an expectant mother's heightened emotions. It was possible that the love she felt for the baby growing inside her was being extended to him because he was the baby's father. And if so, her feelings could change when the baby was born.

And maybe, an annoying voice that sounded remarkably like his ex-wife said inside his head, he should give her some credit for knowing her own mind and heart. Katelyn was hardly the type of woman to impulsively express her emotions. If she said she loved him, she obviously believed it was true.

And he wanted to believe it, too.

But even if those feelings were real, would they last?

Trish had told him that she loved him. She'd said the words over and over again, urging him to trust her feelings. But in the end, she'd walked away from their marriage. He understood her reasons—she'd wanted something he wasn't willing to give her. And he certainly didn't blame her for choosing to build a life with someone else. But that experience made him skeptical about his new wife's professed feelings.

He didn't doubt Katelyn believed what she was saying right now, but they'd only known one another a short while. He was committed to her and the family they were building together, but he wasn't quite ready to drop the shields around his heart—not even for the woman he'd married.

Chapter Eighteen

A few months earlier, Kate might have thought she'd feel uncomfortable traveling with her new husband to attend the baptism of his ex-wife's baby with her current spouse. Now that she'd gotten to know the other woman and spent some time with both Reid and Trish together, she understood their relationship a lot better. They truly did act more like siblings than exes, and despite her initial predisposition toward her husband's first wife, she genuinely liked Trish and was looking forward to spending some time with her and Jonah and, of course, little Henry.

Any reservations she had as Reid drove from the airport to the Stiltons' house weren't about her husband's relationship with his ex-wife but his current one. Though they were both making an effort to communicate more clearly, Kate sensed that Reid was still holding back.

They arrived just before dinner and after they'd exchanged basic pleasantries, Trish shooed the men—

including Henry—outside to start the barbecue while she showed Kate the house and the room where she and Reid would be sleeping.

"Wow," Kate said, after the quick tour was finished and they'd returned to the spacious open-concept living area. "And you told me you married for love the second time around."

Her hostess laughed. "I did. I just lucked out and fell in love with a man who has a very well-paying job at Texas Instruments." She sat on the ivory leather sofa and tugged Kate down beside her. "Speaking of married...how are things with you and Reid?"

There were so many ways Kate could have answered the question—fine, great, wonderful—that would have put an end to the topic. Or even "it's an adjustment" or "we're figuring things out," either of which would have been more honest but still not too revealing. Instead, she burst into tears.

"Oh, Katelyn." Trish's arms came around her, offering both comfort and support—and the box of tissues from the antique accent table.

A long while later, when most of Kate's tears had been spent, Trish rubbed her back and demanded to know, "What did that big stupid man do?"

The question made Kate laugh even through her tears. "Why are you assuming he did anything?"

"Because I love him dearly, but I'm not blind to his faults."

So Kate started with the confrontation that took place in her office and concluded with her declaration of love—and Reid's silence.

"The problem isn't you," Trish said. "The problem is that no one in his life has ever stood by him, not when it really counted. No one has ever put him first."

Kate was quiet, considering the other woman's words.

"His father didn't even stick around to see him born," Trish reminded her. "His mother walked out on him a few years later—which might have been the best thing that could have happened because she left him with his grandmother. But then she died, and he was truly and completely alone."

"Until he met your dad."

"Which only happened after he'd spent a few years in foster care. But even his relationship with my dad took time to develop. And then my dad died, too."

"He's lost a lot of people he's cared about," Kate acknowledged.

"I'm not done yet," Trish said. "Because, if I'm being completely honest, I abandoned him, too. I told him I loved him and wanted to have a family with him and, when he wouldn't give me what I wanted, I ignored the vows we exchanged to be with someone else.

"I did love him," she said softly. "But I didn't love him enough to sacrifice what I wanted to make him happy."

"Are you suggesting that I should give up my job? Because—"

"No," Trish interjected quickly, firmly. "You shouldn't change anything that makes you who you are, but you need to work with Reid to figure out a compromise you can both live with. And working with Reid won't be easy."

"I'm already realizing it's an uphill battle."

"Just don't stop battling," the other woman urged. "Don't give up on him."

Kate managed a small smile. "I'm not a quitter."

"Good." Trish reached for the envelope on the table. "I took about a thousand pictures at your wedding," she confided. "And I had prints of some of my favorites made for you. So if your resolve ever falters—" she pulled out one of the photos and passed it to Kate "—just look at this."

She glanced at the photo in her hand and felt a tug at her heart. It was a picture of Reid standing at the front of the church on their wedding day. Trish had zoomed in on his face, and the smile that curved his lips was reflected in the happy light in his eyes.

"Do you know what that is?" Trish asked.

"A picture of Reid," she said, stating the obvious.

But Trish shook her head. "It's a picture of the groom," she clarified. "Taken at the exact moment that he saw his bride appear at the back of the church."

Kate looked at Trish, silently questioning.

"Most guests automatically turn to catch that first glimpse of the bride," she explained. "I was looking at Reid as he was looking at you. And what I saw, what anyone can see in that photo, is a man looking at the woman he wants to share his life with—the woman he loves."

Kate shook her head as fresh tears filled her eyes. "I appreciate the pep talk, but Reid doesn't love me."

"I'm not surprised he hasn't said the words," Trish said. "He's never been good at expressing his emotions. But that doesn't mean the feelings aren't there."

Kate wanted to believe the other woman could be right, but Reid's response—or rather complete lack of response—when she confessed her feelings warned her not to get her hopes up.

The baptism of Henry Jonah Stilton was a formal ceremony at the church where his parents had married followed by a big party in their backyard.

Kate didn't know if it was the change of scenery or being away from the demands of their respective jobs or if her husband had finally got over being mad, but Reid was incredibly sweet and attentive throughout the weekend. As the guest of honor was passed from one willing set of arms to another and they slipped away from the crowd and into the house to get their bags before heading to the airport, she was almost sorry to be leaving Echo Ridge.

"It's not going to be too much longer before we can hold our own baby," Kate said as Reid zipped up his duffel.

"Not that you can tell," he said, touching a hand to the gentle swell of her tummy.

"Wrap-style dresses and print fabrics are very forgiving," she confided.

"And stunning," he told her. "Sometimes I look at you and I'm awed that you're my wife, and—" His eyes went wide and whatever else he'd intended to say was forgotten. "Was that...our baby?"

She smiled and nodded. For a couple weeks now, she'd been aware of subtle nudges that were gradually growing stronger, but this was the first time Reid had witnessed any movement.

His lips curved as he felt another kick. "That's...wow." Then his smile faltered. "Does it hurt?"

"No, it doesn't hurt. It's a little distracting at times," she confided. "I feel the baby move and I get so excited, I forget what I'm doing."

He kept his hand on her belly for another minute, and when he finally lifted his gaze to hers, his eyes were moist.

"I'm sorry, Katelyn."

She looked wary. "Sorry you got me pregnant?"

He shook his head. "No. I'll never be sorry about that," he assured her. "But I am sorry about that day in your office—about my response to the situation, and afterward."

"I'd never do anything to put our baby in danger," she said softly.

"I know. But I wasn't just thinking about the baby—I

was thinking about you, too. And when I understood that you'd been in your office with a suspect in possession of a loaded gun… I've worn a badge for almost a dozen years now and I've seen my fair share of bad stuff, and my mind immediately imagined all things that could've gone wrong.

"The rational part of my brain recognized that the situation was controlled, but my emotions weren't," he admitted. "And the thought—as fleeting as it was—that I could've lost you…it cut me off at the knees."

She touched a hand to his arm. "I'm sorry, Reid. It never occurred to me that you were worried about me."

"That might've been because I was yelling at you," he acknowledged ruefully. "But only because I was shaking inside at the idea of you sitting across from a guy willing to pull the trigger of a Glock 17 for less than three hundred dollars in a cash register."

"I was shaking, too," she admitted. "And more than anything, I wanted you to hold me. I wanted to feel your arms—strong and reassuring—around me. But Deputy Neal was with you, and I didn't want to cross the line we've been so careful to draw between our respective jobs and our personal life."

"Can I hold you now?" he asked.

She moved willingly into his arms.

He held her tight and whispered close to her ear, "I love you, Katelyn."

She was still for a minute, her heart—filled with joy and hope—pounding against her ribs. Then she slowly eased back to look at him, not entirely certain she'd heard the words correctly.

But he looked straight into her eyes and said it again, "I love you."

"How… When… Are you sure?"

He smiled as her muddled brain struggled to put together a cohesive thought.

"Yes, I'm sure," he told her. "I think I'd mostly figured it out the night of our first-month anniversary, when I came home and found you sleeping on the sofa. That might also be part of the reason I overreacted the next day—the feelings were still new and overwhelming and then, suddenly, I was imagining how unbearably empty my life would be without you in it."

"Wow, that's a much more eloquent expression of love than you got from me," she told him.

"All that matters is that you do. If you still do."

She lifted her hands to frame his face. "I absolutely do," she said. "I love you with my whole heart, Reid Davidson— today, tomorrow and for the rest of our lives." Then she touched her lips to his. "Let's go home."

When they got back to Haven, Reid surprised Kate by driving to the new house instead of their apartment. He'd put in a lot of hours and she was eager to see the results of the work he'd done, but she was shocked to discover that the house wasn't just in move-in condition but that their furniture had actually been moved in.

"I gave your sister the keys before we left," he explained. "She rounded up your brothers and cousins and supervised the packing and moving."

"Everything looks fabulous," Kate said.

They hadn't yet picked out furniture for the baby's room, but the walls and trim were freshly painted. Kate had chosen "iceberg"—a pale blue color with just a hint of purple, because although they didn't yet know the sex of their baby, she refused to succumb to gender stereotypes in choosing the decor for the nursery.

She paused in the doorway of the next room, where her

queen-size bed and dressers had been set up. "I thought the master bedroom was the one overlooking the backyard."

"It is." He took her hand and led her down the hall to the master, opening the door to reveal their new bedroom set—including a king-size bed.

Kate laughed. "You are worried that my big belly will push you out of bed, aren't you?"

"Actually, I was thinking a little further into the future," he confided. "A bigger bed means more room for our kids to snuggle in with us on lazy Saturday mornings."

"You really are going to be a great dad," she told him.

"I hope so. In the meantime, we've got a great big bed and hours and hours until morning."

"Did you have an idea about how we might fill those hours?"

"Yeah," he said. "I want to make love with my beautiful wife—the woman I love more and more each day."

"What a coincidence," she said. "Because I want to make love with my handsome husband—the man I love more and more each day."

So that's what they did.

And this time, Kate had no doubts that they were truly making love. With every touch of his hands and his lips and his body, he showed her the truth and depth of his feelings for her.

And she loved him back the same way.

Afterward, when their bodies were finally sated but still entwined, they both felt their little bean kick, as if expressing approval that Mommy and Daddy had finally figured things out.

Epilogue

As Kate's due date approached, she was more than ready to be done with being pregnant. By early February, she was tired of waddling around with an extra twenty-five pounds in her belly.

Reid tried to be understanding and supportive, and he willingly enabled her most outrageous cravings. He even went to The Trading Post one night to get her a bag of dill pickle–flavored potato chips and a package of gummy bears—from which she ate only the orange ones.

Since the responsibilities of an expectant father were limited, he tried to pick up the slack in other ways. And while Kate appreciated his willingness to sweep the floor and fold laundry, what really helped ease the physical discomfort in the last few weeks of her pregnancy was that he told her he loved her, every single day. And—twenty-five pounds of baby belly notwithstanding—he was still happy to prove it to her.

She left work a little early Wednesday afternoon, because her aching back didn't want to sit behind her desk any longer and because it was Valentine's Day and she figured she should put a little effort into making dinner for her husband. But when she pulled into the driveway, Reid's truck was already there. Apparently he'd decided to cut his day short, too.

She set her keys on the hook inside the closet and kicked off her shoes, then followed the sound of chopping into the kitchen. "What's going on in here?"

"You're not supposed to be home yet," he said, setting aside the knife and green pepper to dry his hands on a towel.

"Do you want me to leave?"

"Of course not. I was just hoping I'd have all of this done before you got home." He drew her close—or as close as her belly would allow—and kissed her. "Happy Valentine's Day."

"Happy Valentine's Day," she echoed.

Then she looked around, saw the vase of roses on the table, the candles in holders waiting to be lit, the bottle of sparkling grape juice chilling in a crystal wine bucket. "This is…wow." Then she sniffed the air. "What are you cooking?"

"Spaghetti with meatballs in a basic red sauce with a mixed field greens salad and chocolate chip cookie dough ice cream for dessert."

"Wow," she said again.

His gaze narrowed on her. "Why are you rubbing your back?"

"Oh." She hadn't realized she was doing so and forced herself to drop her hand. "I've been having some twinges."

He was immediately concerned. "Since when?"

She shrugged. "A few days."

"Can you describe the pain?"

"It's just a backache, Reid."

"Back pain can be an early sign of labor."

"I know, but it's really not that bad and—"

"And the sheen of perspiration on your forehead suggests you're in more pain than you want me to know," he noted.

"I'd say it's discomfort more than pain."

He splayed his palms on her belly. "Are you having any contractions?"

"Just Braxton Hicks," she said.

"How do you know they're Braxton Hicks?"

"Because I'm—" she sucked in a breath as her belly tightened "—still several days from my due date and first babies are almost never early."

"I think we should call Dr. Amaro."

"But you went to the trouble of making dinner, and it's Valentine's Day."

He bent his knees so he was at her eye level, and he could see that hers were filled with tears. "It's okay to be scared."

"Are *you* scared?"

"Terrified."

"You're just saying that to make me feel better."

"I'm saying it because it's true," he said. "This is new territory for both of us. But as scared as I am, I know that we can get through this—and everything that comes after—as long as we're together."

She winced as her belly tightened with another contraction and then, as her muscles went lax again, she felt something warm and wet trickle down the inside of her leg.

"Reid…"

"What can I do?" he asked.

"You can call Dr. Amaro now—my water just broke."

* * *

After that, everything happened really fast.

Or really slow, depending on who was telling the story.

Reid called Dr. Amaro, grabbed Katelyn's bag, then hustled—as much as it was possible to hustle a laboring woman—out to his truck.

Nine hours later, very early in the morning of February fifteenth, Katelyn gave birth to an eight-pound, four-ounce baby girl. They named her Tessa Lorraine Davidson, in honor of Katelyn's mother and Reid's grandmother.

Through most of the next day, Katelyn's hospital room seemed to have a revolving door as her dad, grandparents, siblings and various other relatives and friends popped in to check on the new mom and baby. Reid was content to hover in the background while his girls shone in the spotlight, because Katelyn deserved all the credit for bringing their beautiful, perfect daughter into the world and because Tessa was that beautiful, perfect daughter.

And Reid was the luckiest man in the world, because Katelyn wasn't just his wife and the mother of his child, she was the woman he loved with his whole heart—and he knew she loved him back the same way.

* * * * *

Don't miss
HER SEVEN-DAY FIANCE
the next installment in Brenda Harlen's
new miniseries
MATCH MADE IN HAVEN
on sale June 2018.
Available wherever Harlequin books and
ebooks are sold.

"Are you going to switch the babies back?"

Shelby froze.

Liam felt momentarily sick.

It was the first time anyone had actually asked that question.

"No, ma'am," Liam said. "I have a better idea."

Shelby glanced at him, questions in her eyes.

"Where is my soup!" Kate's mother called again.

"You go ahead, Kate," Shelby said, stepping out onto the porch. "Thanks for talking to us."

Kate nodded and shut the door behind them.

Liam leaned his head back and he started down the porch steps. "I need about ten cups of coffee or a bottle of scotch."

"I thought I might fall over when she asked about switching the babies back," Shelby said, her face pale, her green eyes troubled. She stared at him. "You said you had a better idea. What is it? I sure need to hear it. Because switching the babies is not an option. Right?"

"Damned straight it's not. Never will be. Shane is your son. Alexander is my son. No matter what. Alexander will also become your son and Shane will also become my son as the days pass and all this sinks in."

"I think so, too," she said. "Right now it's like we can't even process that babies we didn't know until Friday are ours biologically. But as we begin to accept it, I'll start to feel a connection to Alexander. Same with you and Shane."

He nodded. "Exactly. Which is why on the way here, I started thinking about a way to ease us into that, to give us both what we need and want."

She tilted her head, waiting.

He thought he had the perfect solution. The only solution.

"I called the lab running the DNA tests and threw a bucket of money at them to expedite the results. On Monday," he continued, "we will officially know for absolute certain that our babies were switched. Of course we're not going to switch them back. I'd sooner cut off my arm."

"Me, too," Shelby said, staring at him. "So what's your plan?"

"The plan is for us to get married."

Shelby's mouth dropped open. "What? We've been living together for a day. Now we're getting married. Legally wed? Till death do us part?"

THE WORLD IS BETTER WITH

Romance

5304

Harlequin has everything from contemporary, passionate and heartwarming to suspenseful and inspirational stories.

Whatever your mood,
we have a romance just for you!

Connect with us to find your next great read,
special offers and more.

 /HarlequinBooks

@HarlequinBooks

www.HarlequinBlog.com

www.Harlequin.com/Newsletters

HARLEQUIN®

A *Romance* FOR EVERY MOOD™

www.Harlequin.com